## by Tom Clark

Airplanes (1966)
The Sandburg (1966)
Emperor of the Animals (1967)
Stones (1969)
Air (1970)
Neil Young (1971)
The No Book (1971)
Green (1971)
Smack (1972)
John's Heart (1972)
Blue (1974)
At Malibu (1975)
Fan Poems (1976)
Baseball (1976)
Champagne and Baloney (1976)
35 (1976)
No Big Deal (1977)
How I Broke In (1977)
The Mutabilitie of the Englishe
    Lyrick (1978)
When Things Get Tough on
    Easy Street: Selected Poems
    1963–1978 (1978)
The World of Damon Runyon
    (1978)
One Last Round for the Shuffler
    (1979)
Who Is Sylvia? (1979)
The Great Naropa Poetry Wars
    (1980)
The Last Gas Station and Other
    Stories (1980)
The End of the Line (1980)
A Short Guide to the High
    Plains (1981)

Heartbreak Hotel (1981)
Nine Songs (1981)
Under the Fortune Palms
    (1982)
Jack Kerouac (1984)
Paradise Resisted: Selected
    Poems 1978–1984
    (1984)
Property (1984)
The Border (1985)
Late Returns: A Memoir of
    Ted Berrigan (1985)
His Supposition (1986)
The Exile of Céline (1987)
Disordered Ideas (1987)
Apocalyptic Talkshow (1987)
Easter Sunday (1988)
The Poetry Beat: Reviewing
    the Eighties (1990)
Fractured Karma (1990)
Charles Olson: The Allegory
    of a Poet's Life (1991)
Sleepwalker's Fate: New and
    Selected Poems
    1965–1991 (1992)
Robert Creeley and the
    Genius of the American
    Common Place (1993)
Junkets on a Sad Planet:
    Scenes from the Life of
    John Keats (1994)
Like Real People (1995)
Empire of Skin (1997)
White Thought (1997)
The Spell: A Romance (2000)

# TOM CLARK

# THE SPELL

*A Romance*

BLACK SPARROW PRESS · SANTA ROSA
2000

**ACKNOWLEDGMENTS**

Selected chapters and poems from this book, some in earlier versions, first appeared in *The American Poetry Review, Big Bridge, Blue Book, Fire, Fourteen Hills, Gare du Nord, The Hat, Jacket, Log, Mike & Dale's Younger Poets, Mungo vs. Ranger, Penumbra, Prosodia,* and *Skanky Possum.*

**LIBRARY OF CONGRESS CATALOGING-IN-PUBLICATION DATA**

Clark, Tom, 1941–
    The spell : a romance / Tom Clark.
      p.   cm.
    ISBN 1-57423-123-5 (paperback)
    ISBN 1-57423-124-3 (cloth trade)
    ISBN 1-57423-125-1 (signed cloth)
      I. Title.
PS3553.L29 S74    2000
813'.54—dc21                      00-23695

*to Angelica, in the Chapel Perilous*

# CONTENTS

## 7. Madness and Exile

# PRELUDE: BLUE MORPHO

*. I do not know whether I was then a man*
*dreaming I was a butterfly, or whether*
*I am now a butterfly dreaming I am a man.*

—Chuang Tzu, the Elder

Spring sunshine
irradiates the stunted jack pine
with toxic light. Time sleeps
for the blue morpho. The wink
of wings as she probes
orange-throated corollas
of shaded woodland flowers
was programmed eons ago

but as she spirals up
to break away the airflow
data mosaics
and flight plan codes
show up on bright screens
in a cool dark corridor
of the hero's dream
this moment *now*.

# THE SPELL: *A Romance*

Riddles appear where there is an emphatic intention to elevate an artifact or an event that seems to contain nothing at all, or nothing out of the ordinary, to the plane of symbolic significance. Since mystery dwells at the heart of symbol, an attempt will be made to uncover a "mysterious" side to this artifact or event. In the case of "profane" objects in the narrower sense, however, this attempt is doomed never to reach its goal. If you try to capture its mysterious side in a description that relates to it as a riddle does to its solution, then the appearance of mystery will last only so long as that solution has not been found.

—Walter Benjamin

The mythical spell has been secularized into compactly dovetailed reality. The reality principle, which the prudent heed in order to survive it, captures them as black magic; they are unable and unwilling to cast off the burden, for the magic hides it from them and makes them think it is life.

—Theodor Adorno

Strange forces at work upon the inner soul
Can make a person do strange things
—Abbot Squayre Dood

# I. Born Under a Bud Sign

# THE HERO RECEIVES HIS TOXIC CHARGE

Mysterious is the force
that drives arrogance to call
down fate — at such and such a time
in such and such a place
a witch touched him
with feral wand
and later managed him,
changing his nature,
making him strange
                    forever

## MADDER LAKE

E ven before they found the body of Nivene, that skinny little pink-haired roadhouse chanteuse who used to sing and play guitar Saturday nights at the No Nothing Inn, all swollen up and pale as a baby inside a wrecked pickup truck down at the dark bloodshot bottom of Madder Lake, there were folks in Central Falls who held the view that Big Jesus Toomer—whose trusty bucket of bolts that lacustrine hearse turned out to be—was just *not the same person* who in his varsity days had led the Central Falls Central Knights to the legendary glory of a sectional championship from his adventitious backfield position. That poor girl was still locked up like a fetus in a womb, with those once-pale-blue peepers of hers gleaming bright as a couple of ruby-colored grapes dropped into a glass of mud, when some local kids diving down there for red-tufted sponges spotted her. An event like this was bound to bring out vivid and black as twisted moonlight the religious strain that still ran deep in that strip country around the Flypaper Towns, stuck together as they were in a tenuous protective band between the helix-shaped chain of Crazy Lakes, in whose spooky precincts backwoods mysteries of hex-casting, changeling species and toxic-spellbound ritual inbreeding were carried to mystical extremes, and the forever obscure Pelting Villages, annually decimated by the fatal lure of as well as the damage wreaked by venomous swarms of funnel clouds. All through that mean, wretched country aberrant convictions persisted in taking root, intertangling and, all too often, dangerously prevailing. Misjudgments based on unfortunate prejudices amounted to a tradition, an unavoidable atmospheric hazard, almost a way of life. And Big Jesus Toomer had either become the object of such misjudgment, as his legend would have us believe, or was in fact guilty of such deeds as justified those folks who now publicly concluded, as they had long since privately speculated, that *that old boy had him a devil inside*.

20

# THE OLD CALLING

Central Falls Stadium, traditional home of the Knights, where Big Jesus Toomer was first launched upon the road of life that led him to the Day of Destiny, dominated the small hill that arises where a fork in the river creates a V of green wedged up against the dusky factories of the Flypaper Towns, clustered together defensively around the rushing bend downriver. From this ancient promontory, the old school anthem hopefully vowed, *We as fledgling Knights, shall sail this world around*. At the annual graduation ceremonies a solemn crowd of old Knights always assembled in their ritual section of stands at the north end of the stadium, gathered misty-eyed beneath the acid emissions of the many-storied memorial sunken mildewed nuthead elms that shaded from the merciless Pelting Villages late summer noonday sun all the upper level seats north of the 20-yard-line on the home side. It is from this noble vantage, their ancient motto stated, *We stand to do great good*. And no heroic downfield march of inexorable Knights went ungreeted by an equally heroic rising upon venerable arthritic limbs of *standing elders*, loyal to the high ideal of the old calling though never unanimously capable of remembering its earthly face or name.

# HEROIC SWEAT

Were this legend to be recast, transformed from its present state as a mock-tragical history over-complicated by many annoyingly interlaced subterranean roots and branches, all going nowhere, into a romance pure and simple, the best place and time to kick it off would doubtless be upon the rolling green and gold lawns of Central Falls Central, in happier, earlier days. A medium shot of the bright, familiar landscape of institutional copse and sward would open out to the smiling meadows of goldenrod and vetch beyond the campus and thence on to a first flashing panoptic glimpse of the football stadium's emerald enclosure, where, like classic warriors' shields glinting in the sun, the sweat-oiled shoulderpads of the scrimmaging Central Falls Central Knights, toiling in earnest preparation for the autumnal league and section struggles to come, would shine with pristine jewel detail in the imagining mind's eye. Heroic sweat would gleam on heraldic armor, as black-jerseyed number 99, Aggro Vayne, the lanky, bright-tufted varsity left end, clapped a rawboned hand hardened in the dark mills of the East Central Falls cracking plant to the argent breastplate of remote, empathic number 44, Big Jesus Toomer, the Knights' crooked-eyed, crazy-legged broken-field runner. The sharp clash would echo across the field, the many helmetted and bare heads of the players and coaches would turn to follow the action, moving enthralled as if on ball bearings, and Big Jesus Toomer, no stranger to noble combat, would fall hard to that hallowed ground, pick himself up with aching ritual grace, shake off the temporary insult to his dignity, and jog back to the huddle.

Yet brightness falls from the air, and, in its brief half-life of being perceived, requires an opposing darkness as backdrop, just as definition requires the unnerving shade of implication, else remains doomed to *say* more than it ever *means*. The obscure lends the clear all its depth and weight even while stealing all its brilliance and acuity. And so it was that over these contact drills in the glittering sunlight of the stadium, the heavy shadows of the mildewed nuthead elms would already be lengthening, even as practice came to an end and the weary Knights, softly chatting or sucking air in reflective silence, rendered pensive by exhaustion, trudged to the showers. The traditional immersion of the violent sporting *rubedo*, with its inflamed and agitated blood, in the *albedo* of the ancient white-tiled common lavatory, with its several steel columns of dribbling spigot-mouths, and the associated rituals of purity or *ablutio*, towel-flicking, and powdering of tender parts, would be followed in the red shades of dusk by the exodus and dispersion of the Knights to the parking lot and thence, mounting their Furies and Chargers, their Impalas and Darts, out on to the several roads of life.

And in truth to venture thereupon would be to enter what might have appeared to an outsider merely the routine encroaching shadows of any late summertime evening in that part of the country. But it was beneath such encroaching shadows that each of the Knights had been conceived. Dense, humid, bug-infested, static-charged, haunted by the first ominous rumbles of thunder from up above the Falls, presage of the coming funnel cloud season, it would have looked to any Knight to be an evening of darkening promise, of questionable omens and dubious signs. A cloudy swarm of no-see-ums, enigmatically humming up a storm, would envelop the thick air in mystery above the roads; the tiny creatures, perhaps manufactured by spells, would mob the head-beams, suiciding in astronomical numbers upon the windshields, yet in the same moment frantically mating and reproducing so as to redouble their teeming legions even as they expired. And out there beyond the headlights' feeble glow the dark would be full of the spinal-fluid-cooling sounds of invisible, yet more substantial beings: the howls of the two-headed dogs, prolonged and subliminally threatening, and the weird, tremulous hoots of spellbound mechanical owls.

And as they drove along further, coming in range of the great cataract where the weather-vulnerable Pelting Villages give way to the precariously-situated Flypaper Towns, clustered together for safety against the unknowable dangers of the Crazy Lakes, the umbrage would gradually come to encroach more and more, to seem imperceptibly heavier and deeper, until a point was reached where words would not be equipped to follow. That, for the Knights, would be home, such as it was.

# THE PERIPETY OF BIG JESUS

I t was in the course and under the influence of a toxic spell emanating from up by the bleak, boulder-dotted shores of Lake Plantagenet that Big Jesus tumbled into this darkly luminous world, and therefore fitting that by those same shores, upon the sunlit, shadow-crossed gridiron at the north end of the Lake, in a game during his senior year between Central Falls Central and its ancient rival the Plantagenet West Two-Headed Dogs, he rose to legendary knighthood with a brilliant 88-yard dash through open field as the final seconds ticked off the clock, securing glory for the Knights and dooming to another year of shame and infamy the defeated Two-Headed Dogs. Thus began a remarkable skein of exploits. A few weeks later, filling in at safety for the injured Pelleas Smythe-Person, Big Jesus leapt high into the air in the end zone to swat away a fourth-quarter pass, foiling a last-minute upset bid by the Mud Lake Slime Pumpers. That season came down to a three-way tie between the Knights, the Madder Lake Crimson Twisters and the Slate Lake South Mechanical Owls for the Crazy Lakes sectional championship. A coin flip eliminated the unfortunate Mechanical Owls and left the Knights to face their traditional rival, the hated Crimson Twisters, or Pink Twinkies, as Central Falls Central supporters disparagingly termed them. They were in fact a hardy squad, and belligerent to boot, living up to their motto, *Chew you up, Spin you around, Spit out your blood*, which their fans faithfully chanted from first kickoff to final whistle. The championship game found the Knights prevailing over the Twisters in a noble contest decided by Big Jesus' return of a kickoff 99 yards for a legendary touchdown. The Knights went on to meet the Flypaper Towns No-See-Ums for the district title. The game ended in a 6-6 tie. Big Jesus snaked through the No-See-Ums' impenetrable swarming defense to snag a 22-yard touchdown pass from Buddy Vayne in the fourth quarter. Central

Falls fans who had traveled to the game stormed the field at the finish and carried him off on their shoulders into the rarefied aether of twice-told tales.

How was it then, that with each year that passed, as time flowed down the river toward the Falls, and bubbled over it, each new episode of this hero's errant life—pulling pigs, pumping slime, pouring concrete, packing pit-banana leaves, catwalking in the cracking plant, trapping two-headed dogs, re-programming mechanical owls, night-wandering in the old rambling style —seemed a little more depleted of his early heroism, until one final night of desolation in the woods above the Falls when he fell down upon his knees in some bramble bushes, cupped his head in his briar-scarred hands, and wept like a beaten child in a trailer, all through the long hours of the Pelting Villages night? Was he bewailing the lost promise of morning, the mutual love of warriors who die together struggling against impossible odds on a field of battle forever tilted toward the turbid slime-beds at the bottom of Mud Lake?

# BORN UNDER A BUD SIGN

The toxic spell up by Lake Plantagenet on the night Big Jesus was born killed a few old Knights and left a bunch of others *laid up pretty serious*. A whole range of changes in function took place in the protein-coding genes of just about everybody who was exposed, which unfortunately included the entire population of the Pelting Villages area, as well as the Flypaper Towns. Small molecule metabolisms suffered severe degradation in several carbon compounds; energy metabolisms were variously altered, especially in the Glyoxylate bypass and Pentose phosphate pathway regions; respiratory function systems were subject to specific mutations in the nitrate reductase chain; broad regulatory function genes including many repressors and activators would never again be the same; macromolecular metabolism showed significant signs of breakdown in the areas of DNA replication and repair; and last but not least a significant number of cell envelope binding-proteins fell into a state of drastic risk, in particular the heat-shock regulator chains.

Any child brought into the world in downtown Central Falls on that fateful evening, in short, had at best a precarious future.

Most people literally never knew what hit them. Information about the toxic spell was released only to those enrolled in a recognized religious order, at a level of the elder sub-abbot or higher. At the Secret Shacks, due precautions were observed. The general citizenry, however, remained entirely in the dark, that fateful funnel cloud night.

The only births registered that night at Central Hospital, as it happens, were those of a set of boy-twins, entering the world at exactly 3:59 A. M. Their mother was Abigail Toomer, the father was listed as Ted Toomer. The names of the boys were given on the record as Zeke and Big Jesus. Little Zeke succumbed within a few days to respiratory failure brought on by brain fever, but Big Jesus, seemingly blessed with, or as some think possessed by, special powers, survived.

Poor Zeke Toomer was born with two toes on his left foot. A duty nurse whose grandmother had been a witch put the word out he had a cloven hoof. Nobody paid her much mind. The only evident sign of oddness in Big Jesus was his eyes being slightly different from one another in color and purpose, the one a good blue eye, the other a wandering grey one, which his Ma took to be a powerful good omen, though other folks later figured it represented the effect of some specific spell, connected with the memory of Little Zeke or worse.

The hospital happened to be right across the street from the No Nothing Inn. All night long, as Abigail Toomer endured the woesome birth throes, a red neon B U D sign in the front window of the No Nothing flashed on and off and on and off, projecting a small rhythmic reflection of hell on the vomitus-yellow backdrop of Ma Toomer's ground-floor institutional wall.

Central Falls being a pretty eclectic town, when it came to religious persuasion, nobody took much notice outside the Orders when Abigail Toomer chose to name her surviving twin after the hero of an obscure ancient sect. Inside the Orders, it was generally figured that the person most likely to suffer curse as a consequence of this rash naming would be the boy himself. The child who died, Zeke, had been named after Grandpa Toomer, a cranky old moonshiner who was said to be holed up out by Mud Lake after a life of questionable activities. Ted Toomer, the twins' father, was for that matter hardly a civic paragon. An out-of-work Secret Shack roofer, Ted had taken to drinking heavily in the long dry spells between funnel cloud seasons, and had abandoned Abigail some weeks before the first twister of that year hit. Epaminondas the Particular, the official chronicler of these matters in the Order of the Books, reports that this rather enigmatic fellow was never again seen in the Pelting Villages—though there is a small, mysterious footnote in the Archives of the Flypaper Towns suggesting that Ted Toomer may have been a member of a band of touring puppet-dwarf art-musicians reputed to be performing on the hunting and haunting circuit one funnel cloud season out by Lake Insanity.

# THE HERO LAMENTS HIS MONIKER

This name is my hair shirt or deceiving
amputee-sleeve flapping
My mother stuck it on me one storm
torn night in the morning
I wake up strange my sickly axlike dark
stark visage staring back at me au naturel
from the other side of the glass
universe created by this spell

## 2. Gallantry

# WILL-O'-THE-WISP NIVENE

Call that hero a prophet wandering eyed,
that lady a fluttering butterfly
flung flimsy-winged from a funnel cloud
to beguile that blundering knight
into comical questing hexhood.

Call her a specimen—so lucent
under glassine he sees her wings
as the perfect transparencies
all things were meant to be
converted to under sedation.

# PORTRAIT OF THE HERO

Here is a complete picture of Big Jesus some thirty funnel cloud seasons down the line, as we must now come to know him. Hard-staring, cool and true as a rule, his good blue eye also revealed at times the vulnerability of the emotionally disinherited. At least a hint of tenderness lurked there, aching to be tricked out. His wandering grey eye, conversely, had looked on the housing tract, the cheap motel, the bowling alley and the pool hall as its homes too long to forgive the destructiveness of its origins. It saw nothing steadily, and little for which to hope. His brow was large yet his head wedge-thin. He had a hunger about him, which made him appear by turns lean, alert, maniacal, lazy, dozing. He had the long greasy hair, stringy whiskers and harrowed, bony hawk-faced-prophet look of a dangerous individual. But he had a gentle heart worn at the highwater mark of his pipestem trousers, right above the battered old range-bellied red leather boots.

# DOOFUS VOODOO

The first time Big Jesus had his wandering grey eye caught up by Nivene the chanteuse, she was holding sway on the little two-bit stage at the No Nothing Inn, piping one of her own compositions quasi-tunefully into that spooky ether of hers like somebody singing while weaving a spell. It was her signature number, "Doofus Voodoo." Some local kids with guitars and drums they called themselves Hanging Slider, they were drop outs from Central Falls Central who sometimes played for beers at bars around the Pelting Villages—were up there clanging and banging along in back of her, but it was the edgy differentness of the skinny, pink-blond, pale-blue-eyed chanteuse that was taking up whatever little intermittent attention the few lost souls numbly slouching in the dark around her were willing or able to pay. She had a voice that seemed to float untouched through the fallen world of the No Nothing on its way back to the raw aching end of some cold blue moon.

> *Put my photo in the fridge*
> *Like a lost ark raider,*
> *Ice me till I'm cubic.*
> *By the frozen river*
> *Doofus voodoo chills me.*
> *Your burning bridges thaw*
> *The hacking cough of that cold ghost.*

That thin reedy voice rasped scarily against the crackling malfunction of the half-baked house p.a. system, a couple of battered little black sound boxes on which somebody had cranked the volume all the way up.

> *I'm out of control you say,*
> *Peel me off your wall.*

*Paranormal Patrol.*
*Hands up on the freezer tray.*
*I see that blue light flashing.*
*I don't know what to say.*

As she sang she did a funny little swaying dance, like a wooden marionette in a trance, and the blueish-purple barlight made her head gleam almost preternaturally, like a fuzzy pink moon.

*Gray strings of pain unravel,*
*Distant puppet masters*
*Punching their remotes*
*Wire you to the carpet*
*Break you up like shrapnel.*
*By the burning river*
*Frozen bridges thaw.*

Drunks bent over their chosen poisons at the bar and couples scattered in the booths along the back wall were drifting in and out of the song. There was somebody irrelevantly laughing, somebody idly talking, every time the din of the music opened up into a quiet space for a moment. But Big Jesus had nowhere in the world of idle irrelevance left to go. His good blue eye followed the crazy grey one into the trap she set, and both of them got so stuck on her they were wrapped up like flies in amber before he'd had a chance to tip his Lonesome Pine longneck three times to his dry, cracked prophet's lips. When she came to the hook of the song and baited it with vague and ominous implication as dangerous as a vengeful lover's drifting restless soul, it slipped into the back of his head so easily he hardly noticed, ran down his spine and turned the blood cold and muddy in his messianic hillbilly veins.

*So peel me off your wall.*
*Doofus voodoo chills me.*
*I'm out of control you say.*
*Paranormal Patrol—*
*Hands up on the freezer tray.*

*I see that blue light flashing.*
*What's left to do but pray.*

She drew out the word *pray* into an elongated wailing vocable that was at once angry imprecation and plea for solace, directed up into the blinking short-circuited colored bulbs which hung like electrocuted heads above the inert, lumpish forms of the mind-dulled, ale-sotted barflies. Big Jesus, considering things as usual with a thousand-yard stare from the back-of-the-room end of his tether, wasn't really sure whether she was crying out *pray* or *prey*.

# GALLANTRY

**T**railer trash is what some fools who didn't know him had the nerve to call him. Yet Big Jesus' having seen life from the other side of the Great Divide between the fixed leg and the wandering leg lent him a certain aura. He was a true believer whose rectitude had been certified by the planet Earth, and it stuck out like a fish on a pyramid.

One version of how he got together with Nivene, the skinny little ballad singer from the No Nothing Inn, perhaps illustrates this best. That dark, aromatic lowlife establishment was full of rednecked mutant locals as usual at happy hour when this big gaunt Pelting Villages pilgrim walked in. He had a bearded hatchet for a head, eyes flying out from the stoked oven that was his mind like burning coals ejected in opposite directions, and about the low-downest hair Nivene had ever seen, real long and matted and kind of slept-in looking. You may find this geeky, she told him when she got the chance, But can I touch your hair? Big Jesus took her hand and very gently placed it on his head. His hair was all ratty and knotted, just like the chanteuse expected it to be. But it was also very soft and clean, for as a lingering remnant of his old Knightly manners he still kept cleaning products at the trailer where he lived. Big Jesus had earned himself a reputation as a loner, but he was still a former Knight, impeccable in his gallantry when it came to lost girls wanting to touch his most precious assets for the sake of a long-forgotten ideal.

Every friend I had is gone, Big Jesus said.

Maybe it's the weather, shrugged the chanteuse. She gave her hair a little toss in the direction of the dim plate glass, a reflecting wall of brown dust through which a little purplish light seeped.

Well I don't know, said Big Jesus, not bothering to look. His good blue eye narrowed, taking her in as if she'd just tumbled to earth from space. His grey eye wandered off. You look like rain, he said.

The chanteuse offered a half-hearted clearing-up smile. Well, what I feel like is a funnel cloud coming.

All my friends are gone, Big Jesus said. It's this damn funnel cloud season. Drives them all straight to hell, chasing off after twisters.

The chanteuse nodded. It's only us here now.

Outside, a small, mean wind was picking up, and dusk was darkening down. A confusion like the aura of bliss that precedes a seizure cast a tinny halo that hovered over Central Falls' spell-policed streets. The fiery haze that had covered the city skyline gave way to the dim light and thin music of those murky grottos, sunk beneath tenement blocks, where boiled catskulls were served by candlelight and consumed by diners with glazed visages. A cart trundled past, carrying a kind of xylophone operated by two busy dwarf-puppet art-magicians, one grinding out some ancient tunes, the other circulating a brass collection cup. In the black distance the cracking plant rumbled on, insistent and unsleeping. Somewhere further off, at the edge of the woods beyond the Pelting Villages, a two-headed dog let out a laconic howl.

# THE HERO AND THE CHANTEUSE
# IN THE BONE ROOM

I've never seen your underside,
he said, touching the top of one
smoky brownish wing
with a bony prophet's finger
as if to index and pin—
they lingered dumb beneath the stick
figure shadows of the ancestors
immured in the bone
room—stunned, the glass
over the velvet-lined
bone-box cases trembled and
everything fractured into iffy
slivers of irresolute
thinking. Let's keep it that way,
she said, lifting
that smoky wing—suffusing
the dim bone room with her
low-down witchy aura,
an electric midnight-blue
nimbus of cool fire
that drew his wandering grey eye
into the stone cleft of the oracle,
into the agate eye of the mystery
that revealed its secrets
by breaking up into seven amber-ale flakes
of detached riddling inquiry, each
of which in turn refused
to speak. Let's keep
it that way, she said, but can
I touch your head? And when
she reached out he saw her
wing again, which he had thought flimsy,

it was surprisingly strong and
tough. It brushed his bony prophet's head
and he could not speak
through its complex translucent
mesh, a veined
and ribbed netting
that collapsed over him
like a trap. All around them
the ancestors'
dim bones glowed as if
dressed up in a radiant flesh-pink skin
and began to hum
transparent hymns of toxic lunacy.

# MOON TO THE LEFT OF ME

T he mother of mischief is a little thing, like a midge's wing. But little things mean a lot, crooned the chanteuse quietly to the slightly distorted apparition of herself that confronted her in the plate glass that surrounded the parking lot manager's office. Her reflection as she touched up her makeup appeared hermaphroditic, anamorphic, elongated, thin and pinkish-blue. Some glass is transparent and some glass is untrue, she improvised, half-musing. Little things mean a lot. She didn't like rehearsing without a mirror. Actually this one was not so much a mirror as simply the large pane of plate glass, one of four that enclosed the cubicle where the parking lot manager worked.

Be honest with yourself, Nivene, she said to the pane of glass, putting her little things away. This is not Paris and you are not the songbird of anybody's dreams, not even your own.

Singing acts specializing in melancholy pessimism of an advanced psychomimetic stripe could look forward to very few prestige gigs around the Pelting Villages. Most new places Nivene played you didn't really know where you were, at first, but then that feeling gave way to the sure knowledge you were nowhere. Sometimes it was like thinking you were playing the Egyptian frontier and yet not being totally sure you were not still in Sudan, and then realizing you were. Parking-lot promotion gigs could get to be a nasty way of life, especially during the sandstorms that swept through the Flypaper Towns for weeks on end in the wake of funnel cloud season every year. Sometimes the sand covered your little amp and p.a. system and piled up as high as the top of your head, completely drowning you out. Sometimes it blocked out the moon.

She had been paid in doughnuts and she had been paid in sacred animals' blood. The mills of the gods ground things up slowly in the Flypaper Towns, but even so they could not grind this morning with the water that flowed past last night. This particular morning Nivene had been out at the No Nothing throwing back longnecks with that crazy crooked-eyed fool Big Jesus Toomer till way past witching hour. Then when he went on back to his old beat-up trailer to collapse, she dragged herself off to work. The crowd straggled in, and she began to sing, like an ancient child, in that ancient child voice nobody could quite put a handle on, except to agree it *sounded so damn sad*: Moon to the left of me, banks of the Blue Nile to my right, Little fish come swimming by the pyramids at night...

# THE HERO'S DREAM OF THE POSTMAN AND NIVENE

Encountering you over Buds at the No Nothing
thinking of you as a melting pink moon
then dreaming of you as an amber-lit person
at the trailer park
the postman walks in and delivers you
another free choice in the deep
                          octane of language
witches taught you
to imitate mechanical owl screeches
this is what you call singing
robots taught you
to look at you naked
is to
        not forget you

Forget I said those words
funnel clouds are brewing
draw a road
disregard the wolf nose
        that peeks through
that carefully mapped cloud
placed there by kindred elders
forget that dragonfly
may have been human too once
now it's a machine
I tell you
sitting with you in the No Nothing
in the dream
before us a jar of larval no-see-ums
don't look at those eggs hatching pink moons
now you are human too and disturbed
winter wet between those legs

44 ❧

magenta moods of the witches' kindred
words behind the hidden agenda leaf:
the mirror trees

You must forget
                these trees are not you
life swallowed you
the postman should have vanished too
the dust swallowed him
he was carrying my letter to you back to me
you stood before me emerging
out of those goofy trees with him
("additional postage is required")
on flimsy wings
                        just before dark

# WHERE HAS LOVE GONE

The left-hand moon yellowed down through green from blue as it rolled across the sweat-drenched bed sheets of the chanteuse, who was sitting up alone and sleepless smoking a cigarette in her nightgown in her rented room down on Central Avenue, listening because she had no alternative to the cracking plant's distant unsteady hum, a rumbling rickety-racket, thudding tread of a giant with a stone in his shoe, throbbing tooth, nagging reminder a thousand times a night of what was better forgotten, regrets and desires all mixed up, aching and blunt, words at once lying and true—regrets and desires, a thousand Knights a time—

> *wouldn't you,*
> *wouldn't you,*
> *wouldn't you?*

The mercury yo-yo'd up and down between 99 and 101 before flatlining at one hundred fevered degrees fahrenheit on the thermometer mounted outside the Planet Jupiter, a seamy ripped-fishnet sex bar down at street level, two storeys below her wide-open insomniac window. Out-of-tune raucous guitars and swing-shift pit-banana leaf packers partying. Armagideons Army, a mutant thrash ensemble consisting of four toxic-shocked puppet-dwarves from up by Bleak Lake, staggered into the ancient opening chords of "Wanna Be Your Two-Headed Dog," timed to the relentless primeval monotone thump of the cracking plant.

Regrets and desires, yellow and blue moons, bits of words drifting up all scrambled, animal and mechanical noises, grunts and propositions, aching and blunt, at once lying and true—

> *what woods,*
> *what woods,*
> *what woods?*

She swallowed a handful of globular franchise arrangers from the pink moon-shaped vial on the bed table and sank back on her pillow, waiting to be rearranged.

# FLEETING PROMISES (NIVENE'S SONG)

This late hour in the night of dreams
the onslaught of the past surprises
erasing the way back to the crystal clear cave
unable to be caught by light when I fall
under the deep blue rain slick streets
headlights on the wall throwing silhouettes
older than movies of dead angels
whose marble wings are shredded by raked clouds

# PINK MOON

A pink moon floated above the Flypaper Towns, stuck together like the lids of the pale-blue eyes of the chanteuse the time she came down with conjunctivitis from smooching too much with certain varsity Knights in the blooming springtime of senior year at Central Falls Central.

At Slate Lake the pink moon was serrated by the dark boughs of crayon pines, which scissored pieces out of it and pasted them on the slick flat backs of pit-banana leaves. Broad trunks floated in stagnant water, and wooden boats banged on the wet planks of a dark pier. Big Jesus counted eighteen black slats silhouetted against a peach parfait moon floating over the lake, and then while he was still counting Beauty came back to life and stated itself in the high air over the inky shutdown of the nighttime Flypaper Towns. But still stuck inside his head was the not yet stated, and still stuck inside the not yet stated lay the pale, fleshy seed of the not yet understood Nivene.

# THE HERO TO PSYCHE

Everything happens to you if you know it
I turn to the redwing moon for control
Its small cornstalk fringes slide apart
Opposite ways over bone thought oceans
While the stars come out Confucius blue
Above your small hair smooth knob belly
The ghost of a change happens to you
Even if I don't know it yet
From your crepuscular mothfur touch

# NINE OUT OF TEN

The chanteuse dropped her pink-smudged half-smoked coffin nail into the puddle at the bottom of the beer glass, and as it released a damp hiss, gave Big Jesus a hard pale look in his good blue eye. Another pool to drown in. His grey eye was as usual off somewhere, tagging along after the wig bubbles that drifted around him in their usual unseen yet tantalizing, desultory flocks.

Nine out of ten people are wrong more often than they are right, she said. Or didn't you know that?

I don't know, Big Jesus said, his prophet's head full of nothing.

When he didn't know she drew back. She had a beguiling way of drawing back that reminded Big Jesus of a butterfly lifting off from a mud puddle.

Her name, Nivene, came straight out of the Old Annals, though she'd have been hard put to cite which Book. Her mother was rumored to have been a witch for a while, and was said to have given birth to her in a lean-to in a fire circle up above the Secret Shacks.

The wig bubbles drifted above Big Jesus' head, going nowhere.

Outside the No Nothing Inn, a black mantle had been dropped over the scrawny shoulders of downtown Central Falls. It was a mean cold night. Somebody had thrown sparklers into a hayrick out north of town, and on the horizon you could already see the sails of Earl Pudd's fire wagons flaring up against the cold bluish-pink moon. Flags of Dark Nations were snapping on the air, and the wind had begun to blow for real. On the corner some whiskey-drinking Indians and a puppet-dwarf or two crowded around a trash fire burning in a rusty metal bin. The flames licked hungrily at the black air. For a short while the dead lived and roamed the streets insatiably. Anything might have been lurking in an alley. With a cracked snagtoothed grin of intended chivalry,

Big Jesus knelt down on his game football knee and offered to escort the giggling but grateful chanteuse to his bucket of bolts. Not for nothing had he been made a Knight.

They drove north a hundred miles upriver into the woods beyond the Pelting Villages. In the mutable gas-station roadhouse night she caught occasional headlit glimpses of his profile stark and strange, protruding browbone and big nose of a prophet somber, pointed like an ax into the inexorable cold fire of a coming blood-red dawn. She imagined that ghost buffalo rose and massed on a great dark plain which the woods now hid. Driven from sleep like the recumbent bodies of ancient hopes, they charged into the terrific vengeance of the future, with him pursuing them in her mind.

As they drove along they didn't talk. Once the Central Falls radio stations were out of range he hummed some hymns from *The Lays of the Crazy Lakes*. After that he whistled a few bars of "Over the Falls for You," and she joined in on the line about the mutilated cows coming home, and then took over herself and sang the whole of the Weird Womens' Chorus, her thin piping voice rising to a sharp rebarbative whinny that echoed through the roaring engine night for all the world like the howl of a mother two-headed dog deprived of her pups. Again, it was his turn. Airing out for the first time (well, it was the first time she'd heard it) the Knightly style of ritual vocalizing taught him by Aggro Vayne long ago on those difficult scholastic retreat nights by Lake Insanity, he worked through all the old slow sad tunes he could remember—"Little Lost Maggie of Madder Lake," "Toussaint Charbonneau," and even "Incorrigible Discovery in the Snow," with its strange deep-memory images of the fire circle, the Secret Shacks, inquisitions by moonlight, and the legendary season so cold it was not prudent to turn out to hunt in the cold dawn "for all the buffalo we knew / rose and rode off into the snow / in search of the seat of the soul." "We all know what we know," she chorused. "I used to call you Satan, / but now I know you're an ordinary Joe."

At length the new day coined its gold sun in the east. They still had a long way to go.

# BEYOND THE PELTING VILLAGES

Distance
infolds you
within its dusky wings,
Nivene—              stealth
                    messenger—
Distance
   and night.
                 Anamorphic
               ghost—
insistent form changer
                    mirror
                       curver—
my obsessive quest
implicates you—both of us
so tangled up in my lost perspective
on your switching *yous*—      you
unravel my wandering-eyed net
and tumble
out of the blue
                 through prophecy
into yourself

# LAKE INSANITY

A swift yellow moon loped up the blood-pink sky to the west right after sundown. Big Jesus aimed the bucket of bolts into it for a while, then turned toward the dark north at the Bleak Lake cutoff. Nuthead elms cloaked each turn in the road with their old ragged skirts. The plastic skull dangling from the rearview grinned or grimaced, depending on which of his eyes was doing the reporting.

The chanteuse grabbed the mirror and twisted it over her way to see herself, but nothing was made known. She wore pretty rings on all her precious things but at this point the husk of her body disguised seven nights of hard thinking, not pretty at all. That was done and over with now but not without its manifest record of damage, tiny valleys of fret and anxiety carved out by the urgings of her strange will, through which trickled a poisonous fluid extracted at the cracking plant from two-headed dog parts. That anyway was how Big Jesus saw it, crooked-eyed as he was.

They had been traveling this hard road or similar since the beginning of time. She had ordered him behind the wheel and then she had ordered him to start driving, on the theory that a body in motion will remain in that state a while.

Nivene honey, he said after a while, No offense or nothing. He paused one beat of the buckboard in the trucker number on the tinny little tunebox in the bucket of bolts. Only how come you want to go up in them ugly old woods this time of night anyhow?

I've never been to En-Val, she said. I'm just curious is all.

You ain't been missing nothing. His good blue eye was stuck to the road but his wandering grey eye ran off and dragged back a tattered roadside billboard reading: Brain Shunts Implanted, Cheap. Thubo Thup, W.D. Downtown by the Dead Dwarf, En-Val.

The old mildewed nuthead elms and bald-crowned alders got thicker and thicker over the winding blacktop. Out ahead the bright beams of the bucket of bolts caught up great clouds of swarming no-see-ums, but though the hungry beams netted and gutted a million, two million more were in the same moment born.

That old lake's just up ahead here, he said.

I always wondered why they call it that, she lied. Lake Insanity I mean.

No idea.

Oh no? Then who was it twice told me?

Ah you know the story.

Tell me again, she directed. Up and to the left, through the overarching nutheads and alders, that swift scared moon peeked through. A slanted flash of slick water shone up ahead, then blinked off as tree cover closed over it again.

He spoke slowly, like one uttering grand truths to a child. Woman named Diana Smythe had a ranch out this way. Rich lady. Had a country boy named Furness Yellowblood living out there with her.

Good old Furness. She gave a hollow little laugh. I remember that boy.

Well, one night Furness is out in these woods. Hunting two-headed dog.

Oh I love this part! She clapped her pale hands.

Pack of them mean old two-heads cornered Furness up against a couple of dead nuthead trunks. Tore up his leg real bad, so they say, right down to the bone.

Out there somewhere in the unknown opaque woods through which they sped a muffled howl arose, then subsided into the engine's humming diligence.

Well, Big Jesus went on. Old Furness limped on back to that ranch. That Smythe woman popped him into a hot tub. To heal him up, she said. She went off a while, and when she came back, Furness Yellowblood was gone, and in her hot tub was a big old two-headed dog, instead—mean and ugly as could be. So she had to shoot it, she said. And then there was that bad funnel cloud season, right after that, and the lake rose up and flooded her place out. And what was left of whoever or whatever that was in her hot tub got washed completely away, according to her.

They drove along in silence a while. Then suddenly a blind curve released them from the woods.

Ah, sighed the chanteuse. Look! Lake Insanity lay broad and strange before them, a still reflecting pool for the frightened, confused moon.

Big Jesus steered the bucket of bolts up the frontage road for a hundred yards or so, then pulled off and parked in a patch of grass along the shore. From the depths of the woods a two-headed dog let out a piercing interrogative howl, answered half a moment later by a howl of response from somewhere out near the big rocks that formed Premonitory Point. The moon was almost overhead now, breathing deeply. Big Jesus and the chanteuse stood holding hands, looking at the water. She sighed and half-rested her head on his shoulder. What I can never figure out, he said in a low voice as if talking to himself, Is why I always dream so much about this place.

# THE HERO'S HARD LOGIC

In the dark they talked a tactile
body language, but the message
got all mixed up with the medium
sized moon that calmly ascended
above Lake Insanity, enchanting
every living thing yet claiming
no domain over the persisting
howls of menace that issued from
ambient blue darkness, where
the woods hid mechanical owls
and two-headed dogs of the mind.

I will give up my mind for you,
do every little thing it takes
to push the star of hope across
the dying sky of twilight,
sinking into earth to pillow
our heads as we make love in
the ears of the dead, an echo.
Hard logic in a haze of love
dictates every fleeting moment.
You don't love me like I love you
but you love me in the rise of
the evening star which outlasts
the night you grieve and sing in.

# 3. Betrayal

# SOMETHING FOR NOTHING

Something for nothing
multiple head wounds
prominent bite marks
mechanical canines
howling at midnight
seeking redemption
prey scattered to winds

# IN THE RAMBLING LIFE

The code of service or outlaw ethic of the rambling life operated in a negative parallel dimension that drew to it many a down-at-the-heels former Knight. Big Jesus was preceded in the employ of the notorious outlaw spell-bender Long Lear by several of those fellows with whom he had once shared gridiron glory, including his onetime sectional champion cohorts Aggro Vayne and Pelleas Smythe-Person.

For a while the rambling life offered the confused hero a tenuous pretext for his errant conduct, seemingly driving, yet hardly regulating, his restless search for new adventures, inducing and at times requiring him to overlook or ignore those boundaries of person and property which, by dividing things up, held things together in the Pelting Villages and Flypaper Towns.

Big Jesus learned nature's laws from Long Lear, underworld king of the witch-doubters, thought by many to be the devil's natural son. He went to school in Long Lear's devious darkness, took his tutorial in night vision with that iconic master of nocturnal tricks and arts. By the end of his first few semesters he could make out the tender underbelly of things on a moonless eve, and take his bite. The Knightly ideals to which he had once been devoted could no longer be applied, unless with the oblique spin of witch-doubting.

Those ideals, created by the books and tales of Big Jesus' youth, were unkindly exploited and perverted by Long Lear. Under the latter's malign influence, they had yielded to a sorely compromised praxis. Trust of the heart was replaced by a mutated loyalty which in turn eventually incurred deep obligations and accumulated ponderous debts. A debt to evil remains binding, the legend suggests, even upon a weasel. One who bargains with the devil and then seeks to abjure his commitment on grounds of simple shiftlessness, as Big Jesus may appear to have done, enters his philosophical free agency into the silent sessions of the snowy-headed elders while standing on grounds of slime.

The facts were these. As a front for his primary hex-smuggling enterprise, Long Lear dealt in a whole line of crooked-moon businesses—puppet-dwarf slave dealing, book-rite broker-ing, mechanical animal reprogramming, pit-banana-leaf smug-gling, religious-object fencing, two-headed-dog slaughtering—that started out in black ink and all too often ended up sooner or later with somebody or something sleeping with the red-tufted sponges at the bottom of Madder Lake. He had raised Big Jesus up, albeit by dubious means, and for his own devices and ends, from the humble backfield of the Knights, and a decent if minor role in the illuminated history of simple heroism, to a larger, more dangerous part in the darker and more various shadow-drama of legend.

Another fact, before the facts are forgotten completely: Big Jesus had latterly and somewhat to his surprise come to find him-self caught up in an unhappy triangle of allegiances due to his fascination with his liege lord's main squeeze. Nivene's connec-tion with Long Lear, indeed, was one chapter of her biography he hadn't fixed his good blue prophet's eye on till way too late. And that didn't happen until the night she lit on his heroic atten-tion span like a butterfly touching down on an interesting patch of mud, that night he snuck her out of his liege lord's shackup suite and took her out honkytonking to some of the crazier spots around the Crazy Lakes. That was the night when he began to stalk the witchy darkness in her—and the night she saw in the Madder Lake Funhouse distorting mirror the true face of the howling spellbound prey trapped beneath the enthralled chival-ric sexual predator in him, as the band played and the blinking lights of the funhouse flashed out over the turbid, unmoving, deep blood-red lacustrine waters their semaphorically mixed messages.

# BETRAYAL

The breach of one trust through the acceptance of another, otherwise known as betrayal, is defended in the Order of the Books by the scholastic arguments of Abbot Squayre Dood, who points out that in a case such as the one involving Big Jesus, Long Lear, and the chanteuse named Nivene, the total amount of trust in the universe remaining constant, no blame may be assigned.

The turning away of Big Jesus from his alleged former loyalty to Long Lear and the code of the rambling life, and his concurrent acceptance of a new loyalty and code of service involving the chanteuse as correspondent, and all she represented to and demanded of him as accessory, is explicated by Abbot Squayre Dood in terms of the second-order trust of romance. Most noble if least cunning of the several orders of trust, the second-order trust of romance is described as being manifest only to its participants, who are said to be blind.

The conception of service to Long Lear had indeed latterly come to have a grudge-seeming to it, in Big Jesus' mind. After all he'd been recruited into it when he was still wet behind the ears under his helmet. The concept of service to love and Nivene, on the other hand, appeared relatively volitional, and thus tolerably binding. Also, it possessed the advantage of novelty.

The chanteuse for her part occupied a low platform mounted upon the woman's field of desire (according to the annals of the witch commentator Bava Smythe-Thup), from which she looked down with equal parts contempt and pity upon the ignominy to which Big Jesus was prepared to descend for her sake.

# THE TRUST OF ROMANCE

Knowledge falls over Central Falls
Heavy as a corpse. Breach of trust
Of Romance is a capital charge
In every mythic martyr drama
That drags an immortal net
Over the head of an ungallant knight
And draws tight the golden chain
That encircles his gaunt prophet's neck.

# LONG LEAR COMES DOWN

Long Lear, who thought he had a claim to the chanteuse because he thought he had a claim to everything that had two strikes against it from the farthest and strangest reaches of Lake Insanity to the most claustrophobic cubicles of the Flypaper Towns, came down to the Pelting Villages like a diver venturing into the dirty part of the river below the Falls—the turbid eddies where the toxic spells had killed everything, the dead pools where even the stupidest fish didn't go. He was a man of sudden determination who never came without some clear and present reason, that much could be known. He was a man of dimension who did not shrink from living large when it suited him nor hold much truck with thinking small when he saw a blimp untied and aching to be rustled. The rudest of dudes when circumstances pressed, he was also capable of being the most elegant of gents, as and how things struck his evil fancy. He had cleaned his fingernails and in so doing he had dislodged chunks of terrain greater in extent than the entirety of the Flypaper Towns.

He came like a messenger of fate, even an avenging angel, some folks were willing to allow. He wore a long coat, even on the sultriest of pre-funnel-cloud nights, carried a legendary and widely feared long weapon known as the Equalizer, and put one long ten-ton boot in front of the other, every time he set huge foot to quivering ground. He came to exact retribution against Big Jesus for certain acts of the past which had excited him into a state of aggravated rage, in particular as regarded the chanteuse. He was compulsive, events compelled him, and he would compel Big Jesus to bow; that much was thought to be certain.

Long Lear swooped down out of the woods, crossed the bridge above the football stadium, stopped for gas and a bite to eat at Earl Pudd's Bait & Slug Shop, and then checked into the

Falls Rest Motel, an old two-star magic-deco joint out on the frontage road near where the slime-processing units back up on the pit-banana packing plant. To Lucky Lou Lemke, the establishment's unnerved proprietor, he related his malevolent plan, grimly detailing the dire penalties that were about to overtake the unfortunate Big Jesus Toomer as a result of his disloyalty. He talked mean and he talked drastic and Lucky Lou did not feel inclined to attempt to contradict him, just stared down at his shoes and thought, Lie Low.

The chanteuse had pressed her luck against his body, Long Lear suggested. The consequences were now slowly leaking out all over his dominion, from Madder Lake Frontage Road to the brackish backwaters of the effluent streams that emptied into Slate Lake.

The cold outside shivered when it confronted the bleak weather in Long Lear through the dusty plate glass of the No Nothing Inn: he had that wintry look to him, the night he strode in to claim his dark ounce of retribution.

He wore silvery-black opaque shades and an arrogant barbarian grin that would have signalled villainy in his heart to a mechanical owl. His long leather cattleman's coat had so many rust-colored stains all over it you'd have thought he had been swimming in Madder Lake, if you didn't know he'd spent that funnel cloud season steeped in two-headed-dog blood, and was all soaked through with it, sullied right down to the dark russet leather of his titanic boot soles.

Nivene was up there on the little box of boards that passed for a stage, looking starved and celestial in her threadbare thrift-store finery, with her banged-up old guitar and her faithful bulldog amp, delivering herself of those familiar witchy songbird tunes of hers in that scratchy little magpie voice, while two or three drunks and a pair of smoochers and a trucker or two loitered over Lonesome Pine longnecks, none of them paying any particular mind.

She didn't notice her former protector at first but at the break between numbers she knew it had to be him when somebody sent her over two drinks, a White Russian and a Bloody Mary.

White and red was Long Lear's calling-card color-combination, upon which, as she knew from experience, he never varied. *Lamb to the Slaughter* was his clan motto, and also provided perhaps the only suitable caption for that horrific scene of bloodshed, pink flesh and white woolly stuff flying all over the place, depicted on his coat of arms. But it was too late to dwell upon heraldry, for then she saw him, a glaring shade back by the door, standing like some obsidian-minded slatemine workgang boss upon every ceremony in the legend, to recall to her her role in it.

# PULLING PIGS

These were the lamentations of Big Jesus as he recovered in the company of his scrawny, half-conscious cat at home in his solitary trailer after a long wet day at the pig-pulling plant out on the frontage road at East Central Falls:

O my disappeared chanteuse, O my lost father, O my ancient mother, O my dead brother, O my crosseyed fate, O my friends all gone off one way or the other, O the frown on my long face, O does anyone give a plug nickel? He sat with his gaunt head cradled in his bony hands, palpating it uncertainly.

He was lying low.

Nivene had been dragged off by her particular fate to keep company again with Long Lear, which Big Jesus attributed to a toxic spell. *It busted him up bad*, as the legend tells.

He had been working two weeks at pulling pigs. So far the discoveries made in this process did not add up to the losses sustained, anymore than the good intentions added up to the bad consequences when a pig puller clipped a foreman upside the brain-pan with a hog-grapple and the whole damn place blew up with blood, screams and cries. There was neither mercy nor quarter in this slimy line of toil. Did anyone care? Wasn't everyone already lost in space?

He had reason to wonder. According to the findings of Abbot Squayre Dood, the evil rejoice in the tribulations of the good. The good grieve. Only the strong survive. A generalized lameness of gene-binding due to an accidental toxic spell-burden had affected Big Jesus on the night of his birth. But there were no accidents, according to Abbot Squayre Dood. Now Big Jesus was left with nothing to depend on but every recessive weak link in his clan history.

The receptors of his aimless thoughts were the ears of his cat, which moved like furred radar pans in time with the idle rhythms of his interior lamentation. In that sense, he dimly recognized, there was sympathy in the universe. The cat didn't appear to care about this discovery and began to glaze into sleep. But the vague knowledge cheered Big Jesus sufficiently to allow him to put his head back upon his neck and pour some amber liquid into it. He propped worn boot heels on his space heater, rocked back on his banged-up folding chair, cupped the base of his skull in his hands to support his brain, and allowed the floppy wig bubbles to drift off like half-inflated life-preservers toward a far-off floating mental image of the chanteuse.

# THE HERO RECONSIDERS HIS
# CHIVALRIC OPTIONS

To not forget you once you are lost is like a quest
to regain your respect by impressing you
into the chivalric landscape as a Lady of Romance.
Into this impression I have poured tons of
concrete blood and invisible ink in oceans.
But it is passing deep and can never be filled
with anything but more bloody concrete
and inky invisibility seas.

# POURING CONCRETE

I n he had plunged, as the quest prescribed. This was indeed the most ancient of rites, first on the list of tests inscribed on the chalk-board in the Knights' varsity locker room. But the guidelines for questing sketched out in the Order of the Books had made no mention of the sharp chill of the water, the sudden access of pain and loss of will, the terrible fear, above all, of not being able to swim back up. No one had ever been known to swim back up the Falls. You either somehow survived the plunge and went on to your next test, or your quest was reduced from legend to mere history, and you with it.

The wig bubbles drifted as the river of time carried Big Jesus away up the centuries, through the impossible millennia, past the births of worlds and the first sparklings of stars, till at the far-thest turning of a great arc he was permitted to behold his own existence, with its never-to-be-repeated marvels, clan history, the dusty cosmic glory trail and the awful concretion into dark per-sonhood—all glommed together in the terrifying, intense here and now.

The feeling of pressure in his head, heart and lungs was near-ly unbearable, yet the thrill of the quest was equally tremendous, and at any rate there was no turning back.

He seemed to be falling for a long while, in either a well or a chute, buoyed either by thick air or some light fluid, whether floating or sinking he could not quite sort out. Then for a while he seemed to be tumbling or spinning laterally, like laundry in a washer, before coming to rest briefly in an almost bottomless lake, from which he escaped by squeezing his cumbersome bulk through two jagged teeth of slaty stone, which issued into a sub-terranean tunnel, whence he emerged, dazed and gasping, into a sort of prison-chamber of submerged rock.

In this strange sunken cave at the heart of the world there

was a little beach of greyish crushed stone, on which Big Jesus was astonished to make out three human figures, a trio of boys in khaki scout uniforms, with rucksacks and red kerchiefs. They appeared to be made of plaster or epoxy but were otherwise entirely lifelike. Two of the scouts stood looking down with apparent concern at the third, who was bent over on hands and knees, vomiting upon what seemed to be an unlit campfire.

The scene possessed an eerie familiarity that took the questing hero a long moment to identify, as though he were seeing himself from outside himself, as people are sometimes said to do in transitional states of consciousness, on operating tables or deathbeds, in extremis; his wandering grey eye often saw things that way, but now his good blue eye was doing so. Then he recognized the tableau, with a start. It was a scene from his own youth. The boy on hands and knees being sick was himself. The two boys standing over him were Aggro Vayne and Earl Pudd.

The startling clarity of the vision added to the dumbfounding sense of bewilderment. The wonder of it, the puzzle of it, and the mystery of it, all intense, could be weighed in one hand, however, and still not equal the meaning of it, which was of a heaviness so imposing the other hand simply couldn't hold it, any more than the universe could be said to hold gravity, which is never of itself contained, and like the Falls, must forever keep falling.

Yet Big Jesus could not put that meaning, which existed only in his mind's eye, as an image, into words.

And then again there was no reason for him to try to find words for it. His job was the quest, the undergoing and private decipherment of it. The construction of legend remains for others; now it is in our hands.

Big Jesus had figured out from the events that were befalling him that there was no sort of consciousness directing things now, and further, that there never had been. And he was at this moment, precariously, tenuously, and against his personal better judgment, stepping out on the bridge between the old life, which he was forever leaving behind, and this other, parallel life, where he now found himself as a child, on a beach at the sunken heart of the world, vomiting epoxy upon an unlit campfire of epoxy twigs and sticks. Thus he reflected, in this subterranean world.

It was passing strange. And yet it had all started out as a way of passing time while pouring concrete. For hours on end he swam off on these fantasy quests, performed ritual tests, experienced weird adventures. It was a way of passing time by passing tests in his mind. A plunge over the Falls in a trance followed by an imagined dip in Slate Lake could consume a whole morning of concrete-pouring.

He began around this time to forget little things like phone numbers and dates, to bump into things, to "see" things, especially things that seemed to be stacked against him, and to let things get to him. He knew things were out to get him and he said to himself, You can't let them get to you. Still he let them get to him.

The concrete job paid well enough to buy him a new electric fan for his trailer, to replace the one he'd jammed the Works of the Abbot Uthur Ditwangel into, in a fit of pique, during the weeks before funnel cloud season, when fits of pique were going around the Pelting Villages in swarms as numerous as no-see-ums on a sultry late summer night at Madder Lake. That new fan blew the dense funk of the coming-on of funnel cloud season right out through the starboard air vent and across the dusty lot full of parked trailers in the direction of the little colony of port-a-potties, where on full moon nights you could sometimes spot a scavenging two-headed dog.

# THE HERO MUMBLES SWEET NOTHINGS INTO HIS OWN REFLECTION IN THE POOL OF SPILLED EMOTION

My feelings your feelings so pushy Nivene
just two hunks of wet trailer-park anthropology
There is a world inside you inside this cubicle of tin
and when you run into it time opens up yawning
the hell gate cutting-teeth start to chop
and to you this looks like the opening of a door

# 4. Man of Mud

# THE KNIGHTS' VALEDICTION

Mysterious is the force that compels
arrogance to call down fate.
Men become that which negates them.
Heroes fall from the sky like rain.
A spell seems to be cast over everyone.
Splinters left by vanished torture instruments
may well be stuck under everyone's nails.
Magic hides this collective mischief from everyone.
Every one of us pledges allegiance to lie
with vizor tilted back
out under the hellish laughter of the stars
as the funnel clouds begin to blow up wild
and wave to the mechanical animals we've left behind
to remember us to the legend.

# WITCHES

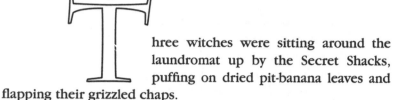hree witches were sitting around the laundromat up by the Secret Shacks, puffing on dried pit-banana leaves and flapping their grizzled chaps.

Parsley seed goes nine times to the devil, the first witch said. Festered nose knows its shame and shows its blame by running. Besides, the devil plays the pipe, and I pay his keep.

She who pays the piper calls the tune, the second witch said. That's only reasonable my dear, since you're out the money.

If you pay peanuts you get monkeys, the third witch said. Or elephants for lunch. No one here is growing wings, exactly.

Nobody blames the sailor for going to sea, either, the first witch averred.

Who'd go to sea for pleasure'd go to hell for happiness, the second witch digressed.

The poor devils go for pay and not for pleasure, the third witch commented.

It is the sameness of the waves that kills them, the second witch pointed out.

Tomorrow's another day just the same, the third witch suggested. Today me, maybe tomorrow you.

Today you, tomorrow me, the second witch corrected.

Tomorrow never comes, the third witch moaned, removing the same old horrid laundry from the dryer all over again.

# THE FALL FROM GRACE

Constant dripping, after all, will wear out a stone. Twenty-two thousand substantiated funnel clouds in the historic period alone would have reduced the fractured infrastructure of the Pelting Villages to glorified pumice had not temporary salvation come along in the form of a gloomy hillbilly in a big-ass black bucket of bolts, roaring around the ravaged, melancholy landscape with his iron steed boiling over and his spurs jammed into the abused floorboards, headed vaguely north, questing like the Knights of Old.

The fall of Big Jesus from a state of grace to a state of confusion redeemed sad cowboys everywhere around those parts from the onus of a victory the council of chicken counters of Central Falls would have otherwise snatched out of the mouths of little chicks still in their eggs anyway.

Every natural person dwelling between Lake Plantagenet and Madder Lake could tell the significance of certain omens and signs from the Old Books, and at this delicate pass, the mere promise of signification itself, with its glimmer of a tacit reminder that experience may reflect more than an endless series of consecutive random phenomena, constituted a real kick in the pants for civic confidence. Big Jesus' suicidal folly in romancing Long Lear's on-and-off love interest, Nivene, his dodgy escape from Long Lear at the No Nothing Inn, and his subsequent extensive acting-out of old psychomimetic-chivalric rituals, courting curse and worse catastrophes, all made pretty good gossip. To those of a traditionalist persuasion, great encouragement could be taken, and meaningful lessons drawn, from all this. There were folks who said they were sure that despite the recent difficult times it looked a whole lot like the days of dark personhood might soon be coming around again. When it came to providing conversational distraction for traumatized victims of preternatural disasters, after all, a fleabitten, mangy, semi-articulate legend was better than no legend at all.

In the jealous hex-world up by the Secret Shacks, where dark songs and spells reigned and the light of reason skulked under a bramble bush, forever out of favor, Big Jesus' name was Mud the minute he stepped out of the great mythic matrix into himself. He was the Man of Mud, anciently prophesied in the Fishtar Text. The witches sent him spellagrams sung by puppet-dwarf, and special-delivery *billets-doux* diagramming terrible ritual cathexes, with tufted bush-bird quills stuck through the paper hearts of two-headed-dog drawings on the envelopes. Some of their curse-blessings upon his memory have entered the records through *The Legend of the Paper Hearts*, a chant work by Abbot Fafnir Dood. Among these are: He shone with a golden two-headed dog on his arm in a pretty glory, he gleamed, he choked a cat with cream, he fed a cat in a bib, he knew a cat may look at a king, he wore an article of clothing that appeared to be a petticoat, he glistened, he was wet: slime covered him, yet he was like the sun: he pulled off his mud mask: a great shudder moved through cloud* like a premonitory wind through a wheatfield: and we recognized him.

---

* Epaminondas the Particular reads this word as "us," evidently based on no better evidence than that supplied by wishful thinking.

# MAN OF MUD

I n his ritual aspect as Man of Mud, Big Jesus now undertook a series of quests. He first pointed the bucket of bolts down the old Madder Lake frontage road till he reached Freeport landing, then turned off into a lonely narrow dirt track that took him north between blasted old stone walls pocked with gaps and rents through which he could make out huge stumps of old sunken mildewed nuthead elms lying on the ground in bunches, as though some great noxious hand had swept through and pressed them down. The going got muddy after a while, with hollows and dips bottoming out into short steep ridges that took a hard foot to the floor of the bucket of bolts to scale, metal grinding and rubber spinning in slime much of the way. He passed a toxic dump tanker heading the other way, rumbling along through the slop on rusty old rims and tired treads. The driver was a puppet-dwarf on a box, with a dark vizor pulled down over his face. Big Jesus feared the worst. Sure enough, just a few minutes later the spell-burdened bucket of bolts began to cough and sputter. The engine faltered for half a furlong, then produced a rending terminal rasp, and he was brought to an awkward halt in the midst of unfamiliar country.

He got out and started to proceed on foot, as best he was able. He followed a muddy footpath for a while, but before long found himself completely lost. There were scrub woods overhead and underfoot a great sea of squishy red clay. He staggered along until he came to a humble shack. The place was dark but next to the back door, which was padlocked shut, there was a hole just large enough for him to squeeze his body through. As he wiggled into the opening, mud and clay squished up into his mouth, eyes and nostrils, nearly suffocating him. He made it through by pressing himself flat in the mud, holding his breath, and slithering blindly along like a reptile for a few seconds. Inside there was a dirt floor, also muddy, a table and chair which he could make out only dimly, and a great mound of manure which gave off a horrendous stench. No sooner had he taken all this in than a loud knock came at the front door, which seemed to be barred from the inside. A fist of terror clutched at his mud-bespattered heart. He hurriedly felt his way along the bare timber walls with muddy hands, trying to find another exit. A blue light suddenly flooded the shack. Someone was shining a beam from outside. The blue light helped his wandering grey eye pick out the small door of what looked like a wall refrigerator. He grabbed the handle, yanked, and inside found a bright white light illuminating a dank ice-fogged cubicle containing a frozen, hoary photograph of himself, affixed to the back of the box by an ice pick thrust through his good blue prophet's eye.

He had been set up, quite plainly. Sad to say, the influence of Long Lear extended an unsavory hand into the dark-time backwater spell-traffic, by way of the elders of the paranormal constabulary up at Madder Lake. Big Jesus realized suddenly that he was not only *in deep* with his adversary but the victim of a first-order *doofus voodoo charming*, approximately nine-tenths as dangerous as a *doofus voodoo rude*, but much more insidious. He knew the rules of the game. He had to think fast, discern daylight, and access it. He visualized a pigskin situation, on a Knightly gridiron of yore. It was third and fifteen on the Knights' own 10 yard line, down a score with minutes to go. He had to scoot back through that hole he'd come in by, before it closed up on him and all hope of escape was lost. A great pounding surrounded him. Just as the atoms of the battered-down front door of the shack collapsed, blasted to smithereens, he dove through a pool of blue light for the narrow opening. He belly-flopped with a great splash and squirted through like greased lightning on a blazing sled of mud, leaving nothing behind him but a slimy set of tracks for the hunters who now crashed in.

By the time his pursuers pointed their blue searches into the squelched obscurity he'd made mushy tracks halfway back to the road. The bucket of bolts awaited him, its loyal mechanical spirit revived by the respite. He lay down beside it, and fell into a deep sleep.

84 🜋

# THE KNIGHT PAUSES IN HIS QUEST TO ATTEND THE CONVENTION OF DUSKY WINGS

And then the mechanical dusky wings gathered,
visiting flowers freely
all over the insect farms,
flying erratic, fast
daylight missions, pupating early
in spring and basking
in a slow season-long larval
growth. Mechanical
dreamy dusky wings haunted
woodland trails and roads
and open clearings, flitting
unpredictably out of the trees
when stalked by puppet
dwarf art magicians
brandishing tattered pit
banana tree bark fiber
nets. Sleepy dusky wings
ranged further south
into the margins of the violet
twilight zone just north
of the Pelting Villages, flying
swifter and swifter
as the spell rays overcame
their systems. Mottled dusky
wings headed westward over open
prairies beyond Lake
Insanity to breed, then
doubled back to join
up with the equally
revenant sleepy wings

which were circling nervously
in waiting. The wild indigo
and columbine duskies
all now flocked too into
a thin flyover band above
the darker parts of the Crazy Lakes,
where the warm greens on the map blend
into the red-orange, grey and hot
pink chill spots marking toxin
saturations. The funereal
duskies paused and grazed
on clover before turning again
to the hunt for a programmed paradise,
while the meridians
offered themselves up to the blue
and purple bruised sky
of high noon above Madder Lake,
unfolding their dusky under
wings up so fully the hazy-bright
transverse darker spot-bands glittered
like toxic gold against
the darkening concentration
of the hero's mind, with
the coming of night.

# MADDER LAKE BEFORE DAWN

Did he really awaken to find the chanteuse standing before him, shining brightly and naked as a bluejay except for the flashing body-armor which glinted in the first glimmering of daylight, as she raised her right arm, the one with the great weapon in it? Or was his waking vision merely an extension of the dark trance imposed on him?

There is no way of determining exactly how long Big Jesus now drifted in the realms of Nod. According to *The Ancient Register of Spells and Curses*, the half-life of an abandoned-domicile paranoia-hex may be anywhere from six to six hundred and sixty-six hours, varying with the intensity of the venom-charge.

He rose, and tried to speak. As often occurs in ritual trances, no sound emerged, but the fore-echo of what he would have said, had he been able to speak, sought through the whole woods for the meaning it might have had, had he said it, and had there been someone there to hear it. The ancient trees showed no concern. The woods bristled with a kind of before-the-thunderstorm tension that made the pregnant silence of Mother Earth that much the more menacing. At length the fore-echo of what he would have said found a home for its lost reverberation, in the upper boughs of a venerable bald-crowned alder. Yet no sign of absolution descended upon the troubled man, even then. *A dark transgression he would commit, / Dark expiation must follow it*, as Abbot Pinhed Dood's poem "The Fall from Grace" so finely puts it.

As in a dream issuing inside a dream, the beauty of his beloved then appeared to Big Jesus with a splendor that seemed about to speak. And then indeed her body spoke to him, but in a curious dream language he did not understand. He saw her as some hideous tender sea-nixie, babbling watery, unintelligible words, and grasped away from her the great weapon. Once he'd examined it, however, it turned out to be not a weapon at all but a sort of slithery limb-extension, like a vestigial fin. He chastised himself for having so rudely grasped it, and blamed his haste on his overly sensitive state of mind.

Suspicious minds find murdering in fishes, murmured a witch-familiar bush-bird from a lonesome pine, and flew off deeper into the woods. Who said anything about murder? inquired a tufted yellow ground squirrel from a spell-weakened pyramidal clump of old sepia vetchweed, and then nervously scampered away without waiting for an answer. Somewhere in the distance a two-headed dog let out an uninterpretable howl.

# THE HERO'S DREAM OF A SPRITE NEAR MADDER LAKE

It's the day before winter reversed
the day of the dead when
here in the mud of the forest
the veil between us and them
is thinnest—and spring's
green umbrella protection
most distant
psyche butterfly till then you'll wait
with your withered wing
folded (in transition)

# STILL MADDER LAKE

W as day actually breaking? Nothing could be defined. The lake was still. The trees were curiously quiet. The wind had stopped blowing. The streams had ceased to flow. Nothing could be defined, but something was decomposing into something. The melancholy of the woods was pervasive and total. The awful smell of mud was everywhere. Big Jesus felt his naked feet sinking into the ground, which squished between his toes, soft and viscous, as if he were standing on a grave in heavy rain; and an old grave, by the rotten odor of it.

Some time went by, during which the wig bubbles grew heavy, and, unable to lift off and drift, sank dismally back to earth, landing on a heap of gnawed bones and excrement. Big Jesus felt as desolate as a slug waiting for the low point of the night to pass so that it could assume human form, haul itself bruised and bleeding upon a wooden beam to which a second transverse beam had been rudely affixed, and drink of the deep cup of mud to which either fate or a spell had consigned it.

The woods slowly grew lighter and the petrified skeletons of some two-headed dogs took shape in a confused heap before him. Torture instruments left behind from some unspeakable rite were strewn about, springs and traps rusted to a dusky hue of old blood. Big Jesus could have sworn he heard someone groaning, though there didn't seem to be anyone around, except some wounded animals, or perhaps they were dead ones; vermin wriggled through their oily, matted fur, and in and out of their gaping red mouths and hollow black eyesockets. They were horrible to look at, and when the scene began to cloud over again, as though it were already growing dark before dawn had even had a chance to break, Big Jesus couldn't help feeling grateful for a small mercy.

# WHAT THE WITCH TOLD BIG JESUS

When the demons inside him had just about completely eaten up his soul, Big Jesus went out and talked to one of those witches up by the Secret Shacks. She told him he had been wandering around in the outside world long enough. He had once lived in the inner world, where nothing normal means much. He must go out now and re-enter the abnormal inner world of his birthright. He must go back to Central Falls all alone, by himself, as everyone else that ever was born sooner or later has to go, and continue his quest. He must see with his own eyes, and smell with his own nose, and make his own bed and lie in it, and conceive of things he'd never dreamed of, and regret it, and burn his own fingers if he put them in the fire, and put them in the fire, and stamp on the fire with his own feet.

# THE HERO'S SOLITARY VOW

I refuse to evolve
into a singer of hymns of glory
for this terrible moon that rises
beyond the onslaught line
where shadows make mud bright
and waves of pink shock
wink through raked clouds
flowing over the violent
toxin saturated ion charged
twister torn night

# 5. The Dump Truck Knight

# A BORN FREAK

Re-entering the abnormal world
of his birthright, the hero goes
lurching off on a heroic quest
which makes him appear curiously normal
when viewed through a funhouse mirror;
but as the flames of love flare up out of
mirror-magic, evanesce and flicker
to expire like a faded sacrament,
normalcy no longer seems an issue.
Knocking himself out for an idea
(this whole chivalric ethos gets old)
he comes to again on a dump truck
and is overcome by moony lunacy,
a midwife of vision who cuts that cord
witches once wove of nature's mystery,
the iron fetters that bind him to life,
refusing implication in his crimes
of projection and anamorphosis
because she has the perfect alibi—
being a true image in a distorting glass.

# THE DUMP TRUCK KNIGHT

I t came to pass during this time that Long Lear put the whole world of his influence around the Pelting Villages, plus the exclusive services of ten ex-Knights in specific, erstwhile varsity starters all, at the disposal of the chanteuse, to do with in whatever way should bring her pleasure. (The doting trust shown by Long Lear in this matter came dangerously close to exposing his ignorance of the craft of romance.) One morning the abovementioned crew of worthies was summoned to her suite in the Wild Chasm Arms, the swankest joint in Central Falls.

In their number were Ralph Dagonet, Kayo Snitchel, Aggro Vayne, Desi Sagermore, Dean Savage-Forest, Hosannah Hardy, Ironside Redlands, Lester Brandy, Dody Smythe-Savage, and Pelleas Smythe-Person.

Roaring Imperial Squadron reporting for duty, declared Pelleas Smythe-Person. You called, Lady?

Warm up your pickup trucks, the chanteuse suggested. I am in the mood for a little drive in the country.

Their route plan was either formulated or intercepted by a hobo with a hot dog fork, who had been seated on a fallen log in the woods for millions and millions of turnings of the stars through those dark skies. When questioned later about his role in all this, the hobo, one Belthar Amboy, professed his complete ignorance; certain fine-print encodings in the *Proceedings of the Order of the Books*, Vol. III, Sec. xxvi, hint that in fact the fellow knew all the angles, but for the moment we shall take him at his word. In the ancient fables, the devil often shames us into taking him at his word when he says he is lying to us, a sure sign he is telling the truth.

The travellers' route (at any rate) happened to take them through the wild hill country up around Lake Plantagenet, a rocky region honeycombed with the ingeniously concealed lairs of several notoriously unsubdued malcontents, unreconstructed outlaw barons and attitude-toting defrocked Knights. The squadron filed at a watchful crawl up the meandering blacktop switchbacks that circle the steep sides of Glob Rock, where one of the aforementioned outlaw barons, Brief Mel Yoggins, had his spread. Brief Mel's pa was Gus Big Magus Yoggins, an old winking patriarch-lord and heavy-duty slime-magnate who for a long time bossed work gangs at the old slime pits down by where the river backs up before it gets the nerve to charge down the Falls. It was an open secret around the Pelting Villages that the epically arrogant Big Magus had wasted at least two hundred puppet-dwarf lives in a bizarre, headstrong construction project: hauling Glob Rock, all nine hundred shifting tons of it, across the Falls via an intricately woven vinebush rope bridge. The greyish-mauve blood of the unsung miniature porters still stained the enormous petromorph when it was installed on Big Magus' spread—which since that time had devolved upon his son, Brief Mel. Need it be pointed out that in the Yoggins clan not only puppet-dwarf life but intelligent life of any kind was held to possess little or no value, particularly when considered up against the interests and wishes of the clan head? Low were the brows and heady the toe cheese of the Yoggins lords, when all be done and said, as Epaminondas the Particular remarked by the by.

Brief Mel Yoggins, though hardly a comely man either of face or of figure, harbored romantic designs upon the person of Nivene the chanteuse, whose honkytonk warblings in a roadhouse called the Naked Mermaid up by Madder Lake had amused him, once upon a midnight dreary, as was told. Now the folly of Brief Mel was well known but it was not great enough to cause him to want to meddle in the business of Long Lear. Common gossip that began in the Secret Shacks and echoed as far as those backwater hills made it plain that Long Lear was currently maintaining Nivene in high imperial style in the Wild Chasm Arms, with her own private fleet of former varsity Knights to boss around as she pleased. Nor was the cretinous Brief Mel so big an idiot as to ignore the Big Jesus factor. Big Jesus was known to be *all busted up over her.* Big Jesus' bale would have been more than sufficient to scare a simple bully like Brief Mel. However for the moment neither Long Lear nor Big Jesus was around. And Brief Mel dwelt almost exclusively in the moment. Fate moreover had benevolently (as it at first seemed to him) landed Nivene smack in the middle of his back forty. Only an insignificant complement of superannuated Knights protected her.

Brief Mel, conceiving the signs to be right for pursuing his active star, promptly gathered together a force of some forty heavily-armed oafs, rounders and yokels. They lay in wait, and as the unwitting travellers came around a wooded corner, burst churlishly out of some scrub pines, hollering bloody murder. Brief Mel's thug army rudely fell upon Nivene's Knightly guard. Great slaughter and carnage befell. At the peak of the action Brief Mel, massive and ungainly, pinned his noisome bulk upon the frail, attenuated frame of the chanteuse, whom he had unceremoniously shoved down upon one of the few remaining spots of greensward not yet smirched by Knightly blood.

Get off me right now, Nivene commanded, somewhat ineffectually. Her words were stifled by the grizzled protruding kisser of Brief Mel Yoggins, which now pressed upon her face in full smooch-mode. She repelled it with a brisk thrust of the heel of her pale right hand, toughened by adolescent labor in a slimepit. Insult was piled upon injury in her mind when she recalled that Brief Mel Yoggins had once himself been a Knight, albeit a mere third-string nose-tackle on the junior varsity. He had compromised the ancient beliefs. Her eyes flashed crimson as she spoke:

You ought to be ashamed of yourself! You are embarrassing these loyal Knights, yourself and me!

Nivene looked around her and saw that her Roaring Imperial Squadron lay bruised and bleeding in the dust. Some who had gone to ground were suffering still further blows where they lay, even as her colloquy with Brief Mel Yoggins unfolded.

Let us hear your terms, she proposed after a moment.

Brief Mel, who had temporarily ceased his grunting assault upon her person, staggered to his feet, dusted himself off, and sneered at the mere thought of negotiating. All this language may be fine, he said. He scratched his belly and spat into the dirt with a grunt and another crude sneer. I've waited all this time, however, he said, Therefore I'll take you as I find you.

The ten loyal Knights now sprang to their feet in rallying unison. It was as if Long Lear had ceased to exist and it was the fellowship of the locker room that now drew them together, to summon up every last drip of force remaining in their conduits. Six were too badly wounded to stand, and toppled back down. The four that remained on their feet were represented by Aggro Vayne, who wobbled forward and offered Brief Mel Yoggins the following words of caution. Few in number, poorly armed and sorely fraught we may be, he said. However we are still Knights. Thus we will depart from breathing before we allow you to lay a soiled paw on this Dame again. Then Aggro Vayne too fell upon the ground, exhausted by the exertions of speaking, while the plucky Pelleas Smythe-Person, who had been down on all fours, hauled himself upright, and gamely groaned twice before again giving way to gravity and tipping over into the mud and blood, landing on the point of his gantlet with a splat.

At this point Kayo Snitchel, Desi Sagermore, Aggro Vayne, Dody Smythe-Savage, Ralph Dagonet and Hosannah Hardy all lay hard upon the earth whereto they had plunged, held there with the weight of wounds sore and grievous. The combat meanwhile had also taken its toll on some twenty of Mel Yoggins' cohorts, and they lay sore smitten upon the ground, emitting several moans and grumbles and other noises of displeasure and dissatisfaction.

And then the battle took up again, and before long Lester Brandy, Ironside Redlands, Dean Savage-Forest and Pelleas Smythe-Person were sorely smitten, and not worth much, for their parts.

The chanteuse now took note of how things stood, and decided to sue for peace while she still possessed power of attorney. She stepped forward, raised a pacific hand, and asked Brief Mel Yoggins not to allow his twenty remaining intellect-challenged henchmen to slay her Knights.

Iffen you are willing to stop over to the ranch for a short visit,

I'm just liable to consider your request, Brief Mel Yoggins rudely granted.

The chanteuse replied with a distaste that was ill-concealed. In view of the circumstances, I suppose I don't have much choice. But I'm not letting my wounded Knights out of my sight. Where I go, they go. Those are my terms.

Well, what do you know boys? said Brief Mel Yoggins, glancing around at his assembled goons mock-theatrically. He let out another contemptuous sneer. Fling her in the back of the flatbed, he ordered. And be sure you mop the blood off them puppet-dwarves of hers before you throw her in on top of them. We don't want to mess up our purty little visitor, now, do we buckos?

The chanteuse sighed. Her luminous face darkened, all cheer sinking into her distant extremities. Without more ado Yoggins' men tossed her into the flatbed upon her several Knights. She landed with a clunk atop the sprawled inert persons of Lester Brandy, Dean Savage-Forest and Hosannah Hardy.

A puppet-dwarf art-magician from Lake Plantagenet, Bufo Thup, had meanwhile been rooting for berries in an adjacent clump of bushes. Alerted by the commotion, he hid out and did a little spying. Once the Yoggins mob, with their captives, had departed the scene, the puppet-dwarf hightailed it off through the woods. Burdened to the limits of his mechanically-defined intelligence by all that he had just witnessed, he considered his options as he fled. The occasional howls of unseen two-headed dogs in the medium distance made his hasty retreat through the undergrowth that much the swifter. Bufo Thup knew the backwoods passageways well.

Back in Central Falls Big Jesus got the jungle telegraph message from a sunken mildewed nuthead elm out by Lake Plantagenet. He saddled up and took off in the bucket of bolts, aiming furiously north. In the purple shadows of the slowly encroaching Pelting Villages twilight the rearview showed him his good prophet's eye burning like a chunk of blue coal in his head, while his wandering eye, lost in a grey carbon desert, tiptoed up to a pool filled with wet light, then fell smack into it. There was a splash. He now seemed to be making his way through reality from a kind of ocular command-post mounted on a flowing pyramid, as he drove along. Hunched fiercely over the wheel of the bucket of bolts, he felt desperate, broken, and alone, yet girded his loins for combat. The wig bubbles swam in a swirl.

Before he knew it, a mist had descended. The unraveling of the narrowing ribbon of road got more and more confused by sharp loops and switchbacks once he got in under the dark shadows around the Falls, where the road curved blind and large old elms and alders lay at each other's feet like slain brothers.

Above the noise of the engine, he started to hear the rolling drums that always signified the same things, the water going over the Falls, the death of the yellow-tufted ground squirrel and the beginning all over again of the life cycle of the mechanical owls.

He sailed in a half-trance past stands of wasted pines below the Falls and then, keeping his good eye on the yellow line while sending his errant eye out to look for the Lake Plantagenet cutoff, threaded his way through a patch of dense old woods, ancient alders and nutheads, before coming out in a clearing where he found himself surprised by a rain of stealthy fire. Thirty lightning streaks snuck across the sky before he could adjust his good blue eye. Big thunder then busted loose. Out to the western plain just shy of the treeline the dust spun where a funnel cloud formed its empty shell. The cloud drew up off the earth, and used its shell as an echo chamber in which to sing its terrible song to itself. Then suddenly it turned and sang to Big Jesus. Just as the noise became enormous a ball of light roughly the size and shape of a potato mashed its way through the windshield of the bucket of bolts and then through his skull, without rearranging so much as a single molecule of the latter. His wandering grey eye had still been out looking for the cutoff when he ran into a world of hurt, and its absence at the moment the hex-ray struck was what had saved him. (*In the eye of the storm, the one-eyed man shall be saved*, is how the old hermit-religious ballad known as "Sad Witches Lament" explains this.) The bucket of bolts however was not quite so lucky. It was blown right out from under Big Jesus. He was flipped coccyx over ulnar into Mud Lake.

He was straggling dazed and covered with mud alongside the road in the phosphorescent gloaming half an hour later when a class II toxic dump truck rolled up. The driver, a kindly puppet-dwarf, saw his sorry state, and caused the woesome pachydermatous vehicle to rumble to a halt. The puppet-dwarf beckoned him aboard. Big Jesus was hurting somewhat; one of his legs was bent, and, curiously, his head felt like it was on backwards; he was barely able to haul himself over the mudshield and flop face first into the squalid cab. The puppet-dwarf stomped hard on the gas pedal and they thudded off at what seemed a great wallop, though in fact their progress was but elephantine. Big Jesus felt like he had forty arrows in him. Can I borrow this truck? he said.

The puppet-dwarf eyed him. This truck belongs to Brief Mel Yoggins, he said. You would have to ask him about it, which you could do when we get to his place. It's just up ahead here. The little fellow nodded helpfully on up the road, which nearly caused him to tumble off the stack of pillows on which he was seated as he drove.

The chanteuse was pining away in Mel Yoggins' bunkhouse when she heard a labored roar of internal combustion approaching. She peeked through a chink in the logs and saw a big ugly toxic dump truck, worn of tread and grime-bespattered, lurching to a halt out front. Under the sign of humiliation, with his gaunt head bowed, his gut hung halfway down to his feet, his spine in a slouch and a gimp in his step, Big Jesus climbed down from the cab and hallooed a weak farewell to the small driver. As if drawn on invisible leading strings he staggered toward the bunkhouse, dripping mud.

The chanteuse called out through the chink, and recognizing her voice, Big Jesus dropped unsteadily to one knee, lost his balance, caught himself, and from a precarious three-point stance declared that he had arrived to extricate her from further mischief and free her from her captor.

Nivene, honey, you just send that sorry dude out here to take what's coming to him, the Dump Truck Knight said in the bravest voice he could summon up.

A padlocked cattle gate stood between him and the

bunkhouse. He picked up a hefty stick of firewood and gave the lock a brave wallop. It broke into twelve small pieces. One of Brief Mel Yoggins' mercenaries, hearing the commotion, ran out to try to arrest the intruder. Big Jesus smote the fellow a gantlet-shot under the ear, which busted his neck and head into two medium-size pieces. Brief Mel Yoggins came running out, and when he saw all this, a look of horror spilled across his panlike visage, as though he desired no part of Big Jesus, whether hale and whole or all bent out of shape, as at present. He unlocked the bunkhouse, fumbling with the latch in great anxiety, and let the chanteuse free. As soon as she came through the door the vulgar lord dropped down on all fours and began to grovel at her feet, blubbering disconnected apologies and begging for a second chance to demonstrate his rustic hospitality. He was shaking so badly his words came out all funny.

Nivene glared with disdain upon the quavering outlaw baron. It was a big mistake for you to suppose Long Lear was my only friend in the world, she advised him.

Then she turned to Big Jesus. A cloud passed across the sun. Dismay began to spread over the bright countenance of the chanteuse. The poor fallen Dump Truck Knight was covered from head to toe in mud. He had vanquished Brief Mcl Yoggins without so much as a blow, yet he had arrived under the sign of humiliation, in a toxic-laden vehicle. Does the legend forgive foolhardiness? Nivene shrank from her savior, the frown now entirely creasing her pretty face.

# THE HERO JUSTIFIES HIS CHIVALRIC SHORTCOMINGS TO THE CHANTEUSE VIA A LESSON IN GEOGRAPHY

Failure of sympathy buries you
in the sand, like the body of
a person at the beach
in your imagination, where
the deer still come down to the water
to utter their spontaneous cries
into the oncoming headlights
of the approaching wave of evening,
that time when your dreams run wild
dogs back into the caves in the rocks
out of fright, and deference
to the way you feel. Baby if you don't
understand I'm sorry it's time,
and I guess I'm sorry too as
and if it's too late to provide
sand castles with
bridges across their moats. Wimps
do that, break
down
into particulate matter, like grains
of sand in the bucket
of a child who remains in chains.
The life of it is in the details,
anyway. That away lies the equator.
Sacrifice a goat when you cross.

# IN A VALE NEAR MADDER LAKE

In a vale near Madder Lake Big Jesus slept by the chanteuse with a small sword between them, and later wondered if this dream was true.

At the center of the forest, amid dense woods, there was a glade where Mother Earth had not yet awakened. Overcome by the toxic spell burden of numberless centuries, she who takes us to her bosom had no time for us then.

The chanteuse meanwhile was still rubbing the last granules of shuteye from her peepers. Was she refreshed, or had she in fact slept badly? No one was there to judge. The great nuthead elms were sound asleep above, and in an adjacent meadow, great black and white lumps, Earl Pudd's cows were fast asleep beneath them, the whole scene still bathed in the fading glow of milky moonlight. Directly overhead there loafed one or two sedated clouds, which on longer inspection proved to be fast asleep likewise, so tired they had lain down on the woods to rest. There were wisps, flakes and bars of sleepy lake-mist cottoning the ancient tops of the nutheads and drifting down into the dark branches of the old alders that grew over the small stream that curled past the feet of Big Jesus and the chanteuse. The small sword—on whose skilfully carved handle the words Little Rift had been engraved by the crafty puppet-dwarf art-magician Toby Nobuth—still lay between them, but gleaming brightly now as it caught the first winking rays of sun.

# IN THE CHAPEL PERILOUS

Nivene, having got her first up-close look at Big Jesus' general level of culture and specific personal behavior, realized domesticity's full house was not in the cards for them, and sailed off to the Chapel Perilous bus depot toting a handbag in which she carried only a toothbrush and a change of underpants.

The walls of the bus depot sloped up to a dark cavelike roof. When her eyes got used to the dim lighting, Nivene noticed that several benches carved out of the rock wall contained seated skeletons that glowed in the dark. The sight sent a cold chill racing up her skinny skipping-stone spine, unable to overtake the heart beats that sped on ahead of it.

To catch her breath she went outside, and found the night drenched in the most beautiful starlight she had ever seen. She felt suddenly unclothed by her true lover, the night. It took her not out of lust, but for life's sake. The halcyon stillness of the moment teetered on the brink of blissful lucidity, then wobbled back over the line into a leaden contemplation of servitude to her sad mission, which she now observed in her mind as one observes an image of mourning in the darkness of a cathedral.

And she went back into the Chapel Perilous, still carrying her handbag, with her toothbrush and her change of underpants, and took her tragic seat.

# EPAMINONDAS GETS PARTICULAR ABOUT THE RITUAL ASPECT OF THE DUMP TRUCK KNIGHT

The part of the legend devoted to Big Jesus' ritual aspect as the Dump Truck Knight clearly has a triple theme. First, it declares the full emergence of the vulnerable and exposed hero. Second, it signals the division of heart which was now befalling Nivene, who was increasingly distancing herself from the hero in proportion as he attempted to compel her attention by his assiduous questing (and the ethic of service itself thus begins to come under a cloud of doubt). Third, it implies the ultimate declension of Long Lear, who, in the wake of this incident, came under a cloud of his own. He was laid up. A curse was placed on him. The Equalizer was snatched out of the air by a phantom woman's hand and spirited down into the unfathomable bottom of Lake Insanity, and that seemed to take the evil life force right out of him, in keeping with the great retributive genius of the legend.

# ANOTHER VIEW, OFFERED BY ABBOT SQUAYRE DOOD

> *A hundred witches humming by the lake—*
> *the left-handed moon of mid-summer rising—*
> *Long Lear and Big Jesus and Nivene riding*
> *in a boat, bobbing up and down*
> *on Lake Insanity—going up and down*
> *together, and then all going down alone—*

The Abbot Squayre Dood notes Nivene's code name in witch talk was *Knightbait*. Her job from the beginning appears to have been luring errant heroes and witch-doubters. And if that were the case, there could never have been any hope for the legendary leader of the stupid (witch-doubting) mafia, Long Lear, nor for Long Lear's arch-rival from among the old questing Knights, Big Jesus, once Nivene was finished with them.

# THE TIME OF THE HEROES

The performance anxiety
that haunted all the knights and heroes
who ever walked the hollow halls of legend
adds up to nothing.
The time of the heroes is past.
The legend is forever but
Eternity, that pure trance,
has the memory of
a damselfly—born this morning—
everything lost to thought
in the swift resonance
of a subtle translucent passing
moment's wing.

# Interlude:

The Hero Falls into a Mud Puddle
Flown Over by a Blue Morpho Swarm
(The Spell Thickens) and Dreams Himself
a Dark Knight of Trapping and Bottling

# I. IN A MUD PUDDLE NEAR LAKE INSANITY

Flown over by a circling flock
of blue butterflies going fast
the hero falls asleep in a bright sun patch
aswoon with pure spell burden
The larval mud bower swells with passing instars
A mothwing fur grows over him
He dreams the dream of the blue morpho
and feels his soul being changed again
when the pupa emerges from the tree line
on flimsy wings          just before dark

## II. WHAT THE BLUE MORPHO DOES IN THE HERO'S DREAM

Changes Shape

Causes Sleep
by quick shimmerings
of its wings

Lands on Mud

Moves toward a silent estuary
where the pure world of speech
forms up into a delta—
an island on stilts
where a big sad-faced infinity
sees as in a lagoon fun-house mirror
its own parallel universe trace

## III. HEROIC ENCOUNTER WITH MECHANICAL DAMSELFLIES

All through the blue morpho dream
the delicate shimmering wings
of the programmed damselflies above
the ponds and ditches around him
kept the hero from waking—
the metallic green bodies
and dark cobalt blue eyes
of the males and the duller
heavier bronze green bodies
and spellbound agate eyes
of the females rotoring
with a mesmerizing whir
over the slim green and brown
nymphs hatching in stems
of plants growing in the middle
of the toxic mud puddle

# IV. BLUE MORPHO'S MYSTERY

Around dinner time
the pupa hatches
emerging from the trees
on flimsy wings
just before dark
(twilight comes early)

## V. THE HERO'S DREAM OF BEING A DARK
## KNIGHT OF TRAPPING AND BOTTLING

Specimen must not be wetted.
Too sharp a point can mutilate.
A rush of intaken breath—
the chanteuse suffers a nervous flutter.
Pinned eyeballs, poisoned sweets
and wings at dusk no stress
release will wrest away.
Yet she slips away—
too wide spaces in the naming?—
tougher more transparent
and lighter the netting
the better. A film of language, then
that won't crush the wings?
Transparent speech, denatured.
Bobbinet, locked mesh—
locked in. Silk or nylon
can be torn, and the ripping
sound of great wings breaking
free *lasts*. So
killing bottles are a must.
A wide mouth tube with chopped
up rubber-band lips—
pinch if you must
but potassium hydrochloride
for clutching her with language
tight against your chest
and liquid carbon tetrachloride
for holding her there, breathless
in an image, *close*—
these are the chivalric toxins.

# 6. Killing Time

# THE HERO SACKS OUT AT THE MILLENNIUM MOTEL

Mysterious is the force that drives
arrogance to call down fate
as if stars fell on the Crazy Lakes
for a reason no one ever considered.
This is the parking lot beyond the blacktop route,
this is the bad translation that loses the meaning,
this is the chasm across which heroes
in their uncertain search must glide
as sure as sleepwalkers
out onto the narrow path of legend,
eager to commit to earth
the dark transgression which will
demand its dark expiation,
to bear the guilt which must
be deposited on a boundary stone
at the frontier between men and laws,
out on the plain of funnel clouds
where dust never settles upon the cold
commandments graven on those stones.

# EXORCISM

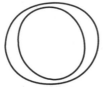ut, out, said the Abbot of the Book. Back, back, said the Keeper of the Secret Shacks.

Cars ran backwards up Magnetic Hill, spell-implanted conflicts of interest possessing their drivers to crush their fists into their own faces and cry out in pain and wonderment. Elders and Abbots held hands with hags and harridans in Reversed Gravity Park, and innocent bush-birds fell upwards into the air as cosmic payback. At Lake Insanity witches in water wings wooed little wooden women to utter wayward execrations, then wander bewildered through the woods with wires stuck in their eyes. Demons driven out of men in the name of belief at the ritual Feast of the Lefthanded Moon skulked off beneath the concealing arms of ancient sunken mildewed nuthead elms to inhabit the inert souls of puppet-dwarves and other rude mechanicals, taking on in turn the several changing hues of the forest as they were chivvied along from animal soul to animal soul.

The etiolated debut of another ordinary nothing day in Central Falls was disrupted by red clouds at dawn that chased insipid shades back into the woods. Large blue thunderheads gathered in the forenoon like great bruises in the sky. At the Central Falls power station two big dynamos rumbled to a halt. People on the street asked one another if the river had gone dry. Some said they'd heard rumors of a toxic spell up above the Falls. Others searched the wind for messages and signs.

China dolls lined the bedroom walls of a three-time loser named Thubo Huggernot. Static electricity made their eyelids tremble. Geese were flying north one minute, then the next winging back to the south. Big Jesus sat in his trailer catching flies. The air weighed heavy upon the Secret Shacks. Those who had suffered saw nothing but more suffering to come. Numb limbs of men in chains in the constabulary bore aching witness to injustices done in the name of belief. Ride, ride, said the judge, twirling a lasso. Run, run, said the warden with the gun, to the prisoner who offered him his back. The manhunt continued. The moon on the wing became a red bird in the night of the Pelting Villages, then when the funnel cloud loomed became the red wing moon. People said it was all tangled up with demons, smelled very fishy and probably radiated either from or around pyramids. In his seamy chamber Thubo Huggernot gloomed over a torn snapshot of the chanteuse. Retribution did not occur to him, even as he unconsciously personified it.

The devil announces his innocence, but he knows all the angles. It was coming up on the season of funnel clouds in the Pelting Villages. Around the Flypaper Towns people stuck together for comfort and consolation, seeking reassurance against the annual onslaught of meteorological foreboding, congregating in nervous circles at the forecasting stations, haunted by doubts about public shelters and prompted by every passing cumulostratus formation to suspicions of demonic cloud-seeding. Another ordinary nothing day in Central Falls, and the manhunt continued. Thubo Huggernot the homicidal moonshiner had not been found. In her flophouse boudoir above the Planet Jupiter the chanteuse (who'd washed out of the Wild Chasm Arms on the temperamental rapids of her discontent) mopped her febrile brow with a soggy pit-banana leaf and languidly punched the remote. The screen filled with shots of demons and fugitives, drowned pyramids, gutted mechanical owls, twisted two-headed dog corpses, dead hobos loomed-over by shadowy puppet-dwarves.

Big Jesus meanwhile sat in his trailer with a ring of fire around his head, trying to decide whether he or someone else deserved this honor. I have always been here before, he said to his sleeping cat, his ritual familiar.

Alone in her flophouse boudoir the chanteuse saw him in her mind's eye when he wasn't looking. There was a blazing ring of fire around his head.

Thubo Huggernot stank like an old shoe taken off a dead puppet-dwarf. He had not washed his uncomely person in weeks. He lit a stick of pit-banana incense to neutralize the fog of death that hung around his head. The acrid smell caused the china dolls to blink back tears. The dim airless room swarmed with clouds of no-see-ums. The china dolls had always been here before. They were impartial, incorruptible, and took an equal view of all that surrounded them in a world they wept for but could not redeem.

# SANCTUARY (SHADES OF INSECT FARMS)

Under unknowable conditions, the bone room
opens for business. We see the pinned butterflies,
the alligator casts, the cow skulls and death masks.
The walls are lined with tall glass boxes,
the remains of the ancestors stuffed
into mechanical animal carcasses
glow in the dark like irradiated skeletons.
Devils gone amok through toxic insect farms
left their shadows scattered harmlessly
here among the dead souls of wrecked cars,
and china dolls said to have wept once
for the soul of a ritual murderer
forever blink back glistening crocodile tears,
a chalky bluish dust gathering over their faces
even within the sanctuary of their protective cases.

# THE RECOVERY OF THE
# BUCKET OF BOLTS

The backwater paths of the Pelting Villages were littered with the dead souls of wrecked steeds and other riddled and spellbound broken things, like the bucket of bolts, blasted out from under Big Jesus by a blinding ball of light in the course of his questing. As many and several curious quests still lay ahead of him, and because the trusty bucket of bolts had always been loyal to him, it came to pass that he hired a puppet-dwarf art-magician named Toby Putho to go out with him to the spot in the woods where the ball of light had blown everything to bits, to ascertain if by any chance the molecules could be reconstituted. Toby Putho advised him that a certain spell to be found in the third volume of the *Ritual Recommendations of the Elders' Wives* might just do the trick.

The woods in that spot had been burnt to a crisp, but shoots of green were now beginning to sprout up between piles of burnished gold pit-banana leaves that had accumulated around the margins of the blast site. A stream gurgled past. Yellow-tufted ground squirrels chortled at play. The exploded molecules of the bucket of bolts lay scattered all around. Bits of metal and glass glimmered everywhere.

As Toby Putho waxed strange and began to mumble and bumble over the scattered fragments of wreckage, Big Jesus killed time by allowing the wig bubbles to drift up into the trees, where they hung like Christmas tree ornaments on the dark boughs. Each bubble contained a face. The faces in turn corresponded to a series of voices he heard in his head as Toby Putho encanted. These were the voices of his ancient mother, Ma Toomer, Nivene the chanteuse, Long Lear, Aggro Vayne, his dead brother Zeke, Earl Pudd, and Toby Putho. All babbled garbled sayings at once. Big Jesus felt his knees getting kind of wobbly

126

after a while. His good blue eye sank back into his gaunt prophet's skull; the whole woods was slowly enveloped in a greenish ball of light. His wandering grey eye tumbled out of his head and loitered off in search of a map to lead it to the place of his conception, a primitive cabin on the lonely shores of Lake Plantagenet. By the time he retrieved that errant orb, the molecularly-reconstituted bucket of bolts gleamed completely intact and as miraculously bad-ass as ever before him, perched like a great black metal crustacean atop a glowing pyramid of emerald light.

# KILLING TIME

The devil inside Big Jesus raged quietly, eating away at him. Wheels of thought started grinding. A turbine of unrest triggered tics and flinches, but a still, small voice told him it was not quite killing time. He didn't understand the inside voices that told him things, but was getting closer and closer to understanding. He sat in the bucket of bolts for hours, thinking about the chanteuse, and quaked and shook.

Who was she anyway? Just a girl. Then why was he getting so grievous and sore? All she'd done, really, was be herself. That, and give him that little wrinkle of a contemptuous smile, upon glimpsing him under the sign of humiliation, when he'd taken all the trouble of mounting a quest to rescue her. Still, did all that mean he was being honorable in wishing her ill? Did he wish her ill? And was he honorable? Who was he anyway?

The vivid strain of atavism that ran through the helical conduits of clan history like a confusing, persistent tracer, coloring with its bright, painful hue much of what took place in that densely inbred landscape of Crazy Lakes and Flypaper Towns, was darkening down inside Big Jesus now, making him act real strange and sullen, the way the devil sometimes does just as he is about to possess and destroy what has come closest to him, for reasons he cannot explain to the uninitiated.

The current eschatological storm in the Flypaper Towns reached back beyond the Pelting Villages to a past when Big Jesus' ancestors lived in houses elevated above the surfaces of the lakes on tall stilts like the elongated legs of water birds. His forefathers had nursed a narrow, often self-conflicted vision, whose refusal of consecutive logic nonetheless lent them in their ritual ways the curiously graceful fluidity of someone not so much proceeding cautiously as slipping thoughtlessly into the future, face first. They glided over rather than descended down through time.

Little wonder, then, given their churlish nonchalance, that it came to pass over time that they became less and less widely loved. As numerous as the no-see-ums that swarmed in clouds over the motionless lake surfaces of summer nights were their historic adversaries, whose name was Legion. They feared the witches and all things supernatural the way a night swimmer in Lake Plantagenet fears the enveloping tentacles of the black-tufted electric stinging kelp.

Now it was funnel cloud season. The glass-bottom tourist boats were out on the lakes at night, and riding them you could see the mutable headbeams of lacustrine space craft moving around under the placid liquid skin. The sky swam all night with lights like diamonds submerged in a shallow plate of tears.

Big Jesus didn't want to do the crime the voices appointed, but looking to the heavens for guidance, his wandering grey eye filled up with the blood of those jealous ancestors, in their ghostly stilt houses, with their dark harborings of secret clan grudges, living too closely together all those long lonely epochs on a sea of mud.

# ENDZONE

Violence burst upon Nivene from inside the imperturbable, ambiguous mask of fate she had been wearing to shield her face against the intense glare of the questing Knight's good blue prophet's eye, which in the fervid late stages of its detached interrogation of her had begun to glow incandescent like the electric vision-orb of a mechanical thrush hidden in a nuthead-elm covert. Was she or wasn't she?—Its insistent witch-questioning pierced her clean through, like weapon. In normal times she would have turned for succor to his wandering grey eye. But now it had slunk off so deep into an aberrant contemplation of his own role in pressing the issue of heroic lawmaking deeply into the matrix of her identity that she could no longer find it, until the final moment, as they lay locked in one another's arms in the capsizing bucket of bolts, turning and spinning and then coming to rest, that fatal night at Madder Lake when he sent her tumbling down among the red-tufted sponges. He had not meant to do it, but accidents were outlawed at Madder Lake by a tattered sign-board tacked to the rusty facade of the Funhouse above the ancient swinging doors of the abandoned laundromat, which has swum in spellbound dogblood in the legend since that night.

# IN THE PELTING VILLAGES

No, what happened was:

His book of angels was opened to him the night he took that gal Nivene, that spooky, not quite earthly, honey-headed chick singer from the No Nothing, out for a spin his big-ass black truck, his trusty bucket of bolts, and she ended up wrecked in it at the bottom of Madder Lake—her pretty pink palms and lips caked against the cracked windshield of her eternal prison, her golden-raspberry tresses flowing like mermaid fins through and around the submerged cabin of the sunken death boat where bubbles fluttered in little schools his flashlight beam lit up when he dove back down there looking for her, his gaunt prophet's cheeks all blown up with stored breath, his hopes all blown up and gone to glory—for if that skinny little chanteuse wasn't precious to him, what in the world was?

The bucket of bolts bucking out of control after hitting a dead two-headed dog out on the Madder Lake frontage road ranked right up there with his all-time ten top misadventures, but for the unfortunate chanteuse it had to be #1.

All over the Pelting Villages the rain came down real heavy that night, and time kind of misted in over Big Jesus. He slouched down the side of the highway dripping and sodden, not caring, sinking deliberately into a clan history he'd never before been equipped to understand. The ghost woman staring at him from the submerged rearview had him tangled up in the uncertainties of his own grey wandering lost eye, while the headlights of the oncoming semi of fate loomed in the exact sights of the good blue prophet's eye that represented the only friend he had left.

# GUILT: A RIDDLE

It was passing strange.
Did he kill that girl? No one knew.
No one ever solved it.
She just dissolved. O anamorphic
moon, say what
this dis-solution meaneth.
Did the stars, like themes
of love and death
intertangled in the clutching
arms of old spell-changed
trees, look down and disregard
it? Like ripe fruit crushed
in grasping nightmare fingers,
deep in the Forest Deep,
in bony prophet's jaws?

The problem of the legend is this:
In the collapsing universe
or black night space
where the whole story happens
you can't make things up
fast enough to cover, or tell
over those expanding lies
the old creationists uttered
of knightly quests, or know
till way too late
the loneliness of the hero
is what makes him a mortal
foe of that Including Spell
which is also the Distorting Spell
thrown over him by witches
that turns the reflection
of a night face into a sun.

# WITCHES AGAIN

The witches were out walking in the woods behind the Secret Shacks.

The first witch came from the second setting of a seventh sun. If the sky falls we shall catch larks, she said. The second witch's wayward glance ascended. The third witch said, That little song bird's dead. She came from the raw aching end of a cold blue moon.

Murder will out, the second witch said. And soon.

Throw dirt enough at the Man of Mud and some will stick, the first witch said.

No moon, no man, the second witch said. Born between moons, Ma Toomer's child, dumb as a loon and twice as wild.

He was born at four in the morning, the third witch said. Night dreams lie, but morning dreams come true.

Dreams go by contraries, the first witch corrected. They only lie to lovers and the blind. Lightning flashed, and her hair blazed with blue diamonds and white fire.

It's the cowl and not the snood that makes the monkey good, the second witch proposed. Thunder rolled, and her gravelly old voice grew grave and deep enough to fill a great tarn of melancholy.

You can't sell slime to the devil, the third witch declared.

Murder will out, the first witch smiled.

As surely as mud will find its level, the second witch agreed. After she spoke she turned around and about, and then rolled upon the ground, laughing and pissing. The second witch turned this way, and she turned that. The air was full of sounds of shrieking and sharp metal clashing. Then the woods fell silent. But the wind, blue, dark and wild, blew away what the third witch had to say.

# UP BY SLATE LAKE

He lay crumpled in a ditch like a toxic rag for six days and six minutes. This was someplace up by Slate Lake, in a marsh outside the Plumed Girdle Last Resting Place. For three days and three minutes he lay face first, then a wind came up, and he was so light-headed it turned him over. His mission and his crime weighed upon him heavy as the brass brain-plate of his busted vizor, yet no one had sent him, and he hadn't done anything conscious the entire time. From that old Vale of Melancholy just down the strip frontage block, with its boarded-up windows and peeling porch, wafted the strains of a girl's jukebox echo-voice, calling out to him in a squeaking baby-doll singsong, imploring him to rise upon his clanking limbs, go off, cross the miniature bridge over the grey Boundary Stone of Retribution and Expiation that separated Slate Lake on the old maps from the black waters of Lake Insanity, and turn left when he hit the frontage road.

# ON THE RUN

Big Jesus was out on his lonesome in that wild weather in the woods around the Falls, on the run from himself and everything. Night spirits of the woods assailed him, bedevilling him with voices. Elements cried out to him one by one, then echoed each other in a soaking chorus. Why O why, sang the wind and the rain. You should not have done this crime if you did not want this pain.

Big Jesus was a true man who when the devil got in him turned into a liar. Then everything reversed again. Deceiving became true and fat hissed in the fire, when the rain drops hit it. Some hobos in those woods were hiding-out in a lean-to, barbecuing a calf they'd rustled from Earl Pudd. Big Jesus could smell the sacrifice. The chanteuse was always with him in his mind now, as the lamb is with its slayer, after the ritual slaughter. *Where father forsook son, brother sold out daughter, devils ran amok, smoke came out of water*: the text from the *Ancient Proceedings of the Older Elders* already applied to him in six of its twenty-seven parabolic aspects, with seven further aspects ominously dawning.

Mists swirled in the woods. Around the fugitive's dripping head phantoms formed up in an unseen congregation, whispering unwanted secrets into his inner ear. He heard muttered incantation, saw forgotten countenances, but quickly lost track of all the sounds, and misplaced the faces. His good blue eye was tear-stained and glassy. His wandering grey eye rambled off to try to save him, and found nine stooped old women weeping softly in the rain. Big Jesus thought he understood that plaintive wailing, the way the chanteuse, as she still lived in his memory, thought she understood the wind and the rain. Buried memories often pop back up as visions, toward the end of the psychic half-life of traditional spells. Joined hand to hand, gnarled fingers interlaced, the nine bent-backed crones in his vision were not weeping, he now realized, but singing. They sang three ancient laments at the same time, with intertwining melodies, and changed expression and tone three times as they sang, from grim and dolorous to tentatively plucky to outright malevolent. The loudest croaking wails came from the dark-hooded song leader. It was ancient Ma Toomer. Her suffering son could not mistake her familiarly abrasive voice. A moment later Ma Toomer's phantasmal figure vanished without trace into the drenched obscurity of shade. The other crones sang on, unsatisfied. Was it just the pained hymn of the pre-funnel cloud-wind, moaning in the tall, sad Lake Plantagenet pines?

# AT LAKE PLANTAGENET

Will-o'-the-wisps thimbled down from an old alder to indicate the direction a doubtful providence had sketched out for him. Influenced by this, yet remembering the past, and at the same time mindless of it, while drawn on taut leading strings into a future that no longer concerned him, he threaded his way through the dark, dripping trees. After half an hour he came to the black lake, with its still, deep waters. He thought he could hear real ghosts singing in that rain. Mighty lonesome night he said to himself, and then foreswore speaking.

He was wet. Water ran down off his head, dribbled from his prophet's nose, trickled over his black, parched lips, soaked into his sodden, stringy whiskers. An owl hooted in the sopping blackness, perhaps conveying a message of some kind. Signals he could not make out whirled all around him. He stumbled along, letting the wig bubbles drift out ahead of him like pilot fish. It was a long, cold, wet, dark night up in those woods above the Falls. For a long time there was no light at all. He was inclined to wish not to have been born, until his ancient Ma appeared again, murmuring his name from the upper branches of a sunken mildewed nuthead elm, and he remembered he'd been dubbed after the honored head of an ancient, obscure religious order, and thus destined to save mankind.

He slogged on. A stunted pine bough hung over the path. Words said by the trees into the night got more and more accusative. The rain knew it and increasingly refused to forgive the leaves. After a long while he fell under a broad pit-banana leaf, which sheltered him from the relentless downpour. He slept a deep but short while. As he slumbered, heart-shaped slugs headed down toward the river, leaving bright trails of slime around him.

# MISCEGENATION

Not until shortly after this, when he was clued-in by a blue-tufted kestrel hunter he bumped into one dark brackish night out back of a crooked-moon watering hole up by the old boat house at South Lake Plantagenet, did Big Jesus begin to dimly twinkle that he might have been mixed up all along in a second-degree miscegenation spell, involving a hex-directed mingling of mechanical and human blood. By that time, in every practical, legal and legendary sense, it was already way too late for his discovery to matter, for his seed was already lost, and the violence of his knightly delights would soon be returned to him in the void triumph of his heroic reward.

# A CAVE UP BY LAKE PLANTAGENET

He holed up in a cave, dead bushed, for three days. It rained on and off. A two-headed dog howled in the distance and a whiskey-drinking Indian played a harmonica. Some hobos and puppet-dwarves came and broke bread and danced a ritual jig around some bones and artifacts that were lying around in the cave. Then they left again.

# BIG JESUS AT MADDER LAKE

here's a story behind every picture including the one those hobos paint about Big Jesus at Madder Lake, where he next turned up.

The devil declares his innocence but he knows all the angles, the hobos up that way liked to say. Now this was a mere band of common hobos, though many of them were travelling in the guise of outlaw *philosophes*. The hobos said they saw Big Jesus come rushing out of a burning barn, up by Madder Lake. Under one arm he clutched a fair-headed young woman with pale blue eyes, under the other a shoe box full of precious ritual objects. Some of the hobos claimed he'd started the fire himself, was abducting the young woman for purposes of misusing her, and had won the precious objects playing bingo at the Odd Birds Nest over by Lake Insanity. Others said he had happened along, spied the fire, rescued the girl, and was returning the box of precious objects, which he'd found in the barn, to the farmer, who was her father. But it was also thought by some that the devil may have caused them to say that.

It later came out that the ritual objects and the barn belonged to one Paul Pulkington-Smythe, the woman was his wife Abraxas, and Big Jesus was attempting to think of a polite way to inform her that he was planning to reinvest the loot for her with a certain puppet-dwarf named Futho Tupp, who was accompanying him. (Tupp's notoriously squashed, bilious visage can be made out peeping from behind the rusted propane tank in the lower right rear of the picture the hobos paint: see Plate B, Fig. 1, *Annals of the Secret Religions of the Woods.* )

Earl Pudd told a story, concerning this same episode. According to Earl Pudd's version, Pulkington-Smythe was a mechanical simulacrum deployed by Long Lear during the period of his ritual detention of the chanteuse, and, due to Long Lear's being laid up, never deprogrammed. Big Jesus, as per his Knightly blood (Earl claimed) was merely rescuing a woman mistaken by his wandering grey eye for a vision of the chanteuse from the manifest distress of being held in embarrassing thrall by a rude mechanical.

# SIMULACRUM CHANTEUSE
# (THE WORD NIVENE)

To not forget you helps me live. It's for
this virtual reality you I fell head first
into irrationalism, as if a foolish little
crime spree, performed for a simulacrum,
were the same thing as a heroic quest.
Nothing's ever linked with anything or for
anything. I fear heroism's a thing of the past.
This is what sex is like in virtual reality prison,
expelled from the kingdom of human time,
my seven-year sentence commuted to a word
I employed like a key that swung iron
doors open so that I glimpsed green vistas,
birds, sky, sun, stars and a simulacrum
Nivene whose face was turned away toward...
what?

# WHAT HE HAD DONE

The legend suggests a spell may have got into Big Jesus. The devil himself may have got into him, according to no less authoritative a commentator than Abbot Squayre Dood. Some may say what some may say.

Big Jesus encountered mechanical phantom species in the wind and the rain and in the pure white moonlight. He set out with a whiskey-drinking Indian and a puppet-dwarf, went down around Mud Lake and rustled several protected specimens of those same phantom species. And when the mechanical who was tending those phantom species, one Paul Smythe, came forth to defend them, Big Jesus smote the fellow upside the helmet with such a buffet that the stroke carved the head, as if it were a state, into two bodies, which met henceforth in separate chambers. And word of this got back to the Pelting Villages, and stuck to the walls of the Flypaper Towns.

# THE CRIME SPREE

I n the waning days of the year 49 by Pelting Villages calendrical reckoning one Thomas Smythe, proprietor of the Slate Lake district, accused a certain shiftless wandering rounder of Big Jesus' general description of theft of goods and chattel, including fifteen large scraps of stale elm-nut bread, a bundle of pit-banana leaves, a trained yellow-tufted ground squirrel, and the ritually-embalmed remains of a deprogrammed puppet-dwarf named Obaz Thup.

Not long afterward, in the early weeks of the year 50, a fellow of like appearance, rumored in local folklore to have ridden in on a dark wave of spells pulsating on radio waves from the other side of the seventh setting of a second sun, was blamed for a robbery, a theft, two cattle-raids, some extortions, a rape, and an attempted murder. According to the indictment, the perpetrator lay in wait with several other malefactors, including a whiskey-drinking Indian and a puppet-dwarf, for the purpose of murdering one Norman Smythe of Mud Lake; he feloniously assaulted one Joan Smythe-Person of Lake Plantagenet, and stole some property, including a mechanical owl, belonging to her husband Hugh Smythe-Person; he made a return visit to Hugh Smythe-Person's place, and repeated both offenses, this time making off with some ritual objects; he extorted money from Margaret Kyng-Smythe and William Hales-Thup within the town limits of Freeport, and a few days later dealt in like fashion in the same principality with Anorex Mylner-Smythe.

A separate indictment of the same period holds the same miscreant responsible for laying waste to the cattle gate at the north end of Bleak Lake. With the help of five other individuals, he allegedly extorted seven two-headed dogs, eleven mechanical owls, 27 sheep in a cart, a cow and a pair of puppet-dwarves from William Rung-Smythe and William Stair-Ladder of Madder Lake.

Another document states that at about the same time the same villain broke into a witches' sanctuary at Slate Lake, carried off six plaster-of-paris does, and inflicted considerable damage on religious property. He was also implicated in a number of other violations of religious privilege, leading eventually to an arrest. On the Ides of the Month of the Dog in the year 50, a character of Big Jesus' appearance was taken into custody as a result of a dispute with the officers of sacrifice at Slate Lake Priory. Two days after being delivered into custody he escaped by swimming across the dank, chilly lake. Soon afterwards, it was charged, the identical culprit broke into the Abbey of Dark Doctors at Slate Lake, staving in its doors with an exploding propane tank rigged up on a makeshift cart, opened two of the Chests of the Covenant, and stole various *jocalia* and *ornamenta*, as well as some sex toys and a burlap sack containing three pounds of sacred ashes. The next day the same fellow repeated the assault with the help of numerous accomplices, broke eighteen doors, insulted the Abbot by looking him directly in the face, and ripped several holy texts into little shreds.

Taken into custody a second time for questioning, the man evidently went into religious detention; he at any rate disappeared from sight until at least the middle of the following year. Just before funnel cloud season, however, he was obviously at liberty, for an entry in the Pelting Villages patent rolls from that time records a directive issued to detain him to answer certain charges.

He took advantage of his freedom to carry off some oxen from a cow shack near Madder Lake. Shortly thereafter, along with an accomplice, he entered the grounds and buildings of the Redwing Tiltball Parlor at Odd Birds Inlet on Lake Plantagenet for the purpose of stealing a pickup truck loaded with six cases of tiltball products. Foiled in this attempt by a pack of hounds unleashed upon him by the owner, one Katherine Paintoe-Smythe, he turned up the following week at the Agency of Strong Feeling in Lake Plantagenet, filed a false emotional claim, and while on the grounds made off with a vehicle belonging to Thomas Big Kick of West Lake Plantagenet. He drove it into the woods outside town and wrecked it, then returned to town and stole a second vehicle, this one a hearse registered to Thomas Street-Smythe of Mud Lake, an undertaker who was picking up a corpse at the Hall of Sacrifices. This great sleek-sided black death-chariot was soon to be employed by the same perpetrator in ramming, whether purposely or not it was impossible to say, into and through the front door of one William Green-Smythe of Goose Field Estates, a Professor of Paradox at the College of Flypaper Towns. As Big Jesus had once spent two and a half weeks asleep in a class taught by the plaintiff, connections were bound to be drawn tighter and tighter, like the golden leading strings by which forces beyond his control were guiding him, all through this part of the tale.

# TWANG

**T**wang went the golden heartstrings, when the witches plucked them.

The witches in charge of Big Jesus' case consulted the Old Elders and the Abbot of the Books. They sacrificed a two-headed dog and fed the blood to a puppet-dwarf named Ethpor Thup, who foamed up several prophecies, each one passing strange, hardly helping matters.

Big Jesus skulked and hid and ate from garbage cans and snuck up behind the interrogation yards of religious residences and surreptitiously listened and observed.

# WHAT BIG JESUS SAW IN THE
# PARKING LOT BEHIND THE
# SECRET SHACKS

Gosharootie, sang the tormented puppet-dwarf, Buthtoe Thub.

A witch had the poor creature hung upside down by the heels and was torturing him by making him say certain things over and over. He was bleeding from various orifices.

Broke, hungry, ragged and dirty, Big Jesus had stumbled into the parking lot behind the Secret Shacks. He was in the act of extricating some elderberry cakes from what might have appeared (to a blind person) to be a trash bin but was actually a refrigerated storage unit, when he heard voices. He investigated. The puppet-dwarf was being terribly mistreated but didn't seem to mind it. Big Jesus wondered at that.

I've got blood in my eyes, the puppet-dwarf said after a while. Can we stop now? The little fellow said this cheerfully enough, but Big Jesus started to get the impression of a clear and present desire to leave off.

Say Gosharootie again, said the witches, taunting and tormenting. Say it, or else.

Gosharootie, uttered the puppet-dwarf obediently. His face broke into a terrible pained ecstatic smile. Crimson rivulets streamed from his strangely large round eyes like tears.

Big Jesus had happened into a training session of art-magician's school.

Okay, said the witches. Now say Thylvia Platho.

Big Jesus could stand no more knowledge of this dark business and slunk off into a dump of bramble bushes at the edge of the compound, where he lay back a while to get his breath.

# THE MANHUNT

One night thunder cracked just as the quiet lanky figure of a man appeared in the doorway of the Moonshine Queen, a dismal lowdown dive out on the Madder Lake frontage road. Nivene had once done some singing there. The stage was dark and silent now. Pleasant enough little gal, the proprietor recalled when asked, If a little edgy. Friend of yours, pal? The lanky figure sighed and turned away.

While it rained six days and six nights at Madder Lake, turning those blood-colored waters a muddy pink, Big Jesus paced the floor of his hideaway haven in the damp, airless attic of the Moonshine Queen and debated his next move.

Time started to stretch out a little and the strings tightened. He heard a voice calling him out of his dreams. He reigned in the wig bubbles. The time had come to move on.

He went down to the Flypaper Towns, all stuck together on that one long thin strip of land that does its best to lift the people up out of the slime, though clan history and religion always pull them back down. But there was nothing there for him to hide behind now, and once again he moved on.

About this time folks who lived up by the cracking plant started coming down with nasty shaking fits. A faint fetid aroma permeated the contaminated atmosphere, and wisps of purplish-yellow smoke trickled periodically from the disused stacks of the plant like the random thoughts of some remote non-intervening deity. The plant covered up the results of chemical testing of downstream effluent samples taken at Bird O'Doom Viaduct, just below the Falls. At first it was thought of as strictly a local problem. Heavy clouds formed and violently broke above the lakes. A man alone unto himself stood out as a stark shadow in the toxic rain that fell all over the Pelting Villages, spreading its misty, soiled skirts from night into day, interpenetrating all those porous spaces time no longer differentiated.

Big Jesus stuck pins, nails and sprigs of rosemary into his arms to keep awake and expel vestigial desires as he roamed all around the Pelting Villages from spellbound low farms and sheep-cotes awash with floppy spell-damaged sheep to spell-mills run by mindless mechanical mole-rats, thinking—so as to cheer and nerve himself for whatever final few ineffectual flailings might still be hanging over from his long-forgotten quest, remaining to be gone through—that continually taking in new experiences was the one way left to keep one's mind free. But from those legendary spills up above the Falls eons ago on down through old time, with its horribly involving electromagnetic coils, no one who roamed that murky country around the Pelting Villages was ever free.

He went up to Freeport on Mud Lake to escape the hunt, broke into a closed-down lakeside roadhouse and holed up there for two or three weeks, but found that no port on earth is free. Before leaving he lit a precious candle, burned a golden pine cone, and made several ritual vows, for purposes of spell-proofing.

I will elf all my hair in knots if I have to, he vowed. I will sleep on pine cones, grime my face with filth and dress up as random patches of simple earthen landscape. I will live as a tick upon a hick from hell if I have to, so as to survive. This night will be my farewell to civilization. Outside the darkened roadhouse, heat lightning streaked across the black Pelting Villages sky.

From the spellbound low farms, sheep cotes and mills, machinery as far off as the Flypaper Towns could be heard expiring. As the mechanical noise died away, silence could be felt coming on like a vigilante, creeping into every potential hiding place, advancing in every concealed brake and covert, covering up manholes, locking down storm doors, filling everything hollow or empty with a stealthy presence that gnawed on the mind, broken only by the occasional lonely cry of a two-headed dog off in the woods somewhere, as quietly in the night the fugitive moved on.

150 🌀

# A SPELL FALLS OVER THE LAKE COUNTRY
# NORTH OF THE FALLS

Blue black lightning streaks the sky of lowering grey
        as in a religious service,

great sucking funnels touch
        down as the Spell falls.

Who are they, then, these several
        characters, and where

are they going: Seemingly diverging yet closing
        in on the flaying zone

where all fall on their knees together,
        resistless prey

to the torture instruments. Mischief
        is collective in these Crazy

Lakes of witches and transgression,
        voodoo, love, and mud.

Escape seems impossible. Woods are the lost
        refuge of madness evading shame,

knights becoming what negates them,
        traditional symbols

of perversity bent and chained
        one to another, shuffling along

no longer able to raise their heads
        under the burden of

what is.

# 7. Madness and Exile

# THE WAY BACK

All that atmosphere charged with toxin
all that water-moccasin stained
river of hate the hero onward rode
released him from obligation,
with its strange cortege of misnomers,
having lost his way back to hummingbird farm,
torn wings scattered everywhere
amid an inane chattering of rude mechanicals
who have turned time to their weird advantage.
Embarrassment replaces animus,
recrimination homeward slinks
to turn against itself and its own,
but who cares how things end up in a paradise
in which hands should fly up to ward
off the insistent patter of isotopes,
face should point out into elements
contrived by witches to warp and neck
should peel back to allow head to drink in black stars?

# THE RITUAL SCORN GREETING

Big Jesus appeared to have disembarked not only from society but from his skull. All that remained of him was his Knightly soul and that too had grown stringy-haired and glowering, mangy and malodorous. As he slunk along through the repulsive underbrush he grumbled and growled, slurring his words together as though they were distasteful to him. It had become difficult to make out what he was saying, or even whether he was talking at all, or just making odd noises. In the backwater woods up above the Falls, that last refuge of the unacceptable and the accused, however, none of this was necessarily to be held against him. His rustication would be ceremonial and impersonal, according to the laws of the woods.

A puppet-dwarf and a yellow-tufted ground squirrel were disputing over a bit of meditating turf, on the day Big Jesus stumbled onto the scene. He was shocked not a little to find himself rudely upbraided, though in a jocular fashion, by both parties. But ritual greeting-scorn was a rule of these wild places, as he would come to understand with time. His rough welcoming committee wasted no time in beginning to familiarize him with the custom by cascading insults and rebukes upon his unassuming person.

Boxhead! the puppet-dwarf shouted into his gaunt prophet's visage.

Hairface! chattered the yellow-tufted squirrel.

Meagrewit! chanted the puppet-dwarf, and so on. (Ref. Epaminondas the Particular, *Life of Big Jesus*, III. 116.)

# INTELLECTUAL HISTORY
# OF THE WOODS

Much of what Big Jesus learned in his period of madness and exile came, not inappropriately, from those roaming mental pygmies of the place, the puppet-dwarves, whose situation in so many ways reflected his own.

To be jerked around on invisible leading strings, tugged, shaken, compelled, until the mechanical dance of life seemed strange and unreal, was the common fate of those helpless creatures, who became aware only just before death that they had never really been given a faculty of choice, and had merely been deceived all along into believing they were acting freely. By that time of course it was too late for them to start over again, to do things in a different way, for their own reasons rather than those they mistakenly thought they had chosen. Bitter salt tears of betrayal welled up in their sad round eyes, then, as they stared unseeing into the uncaring faces of the puppetmistresses and puppetmasters who had manipulated them for evil ends, and now were letting them go.

Every now and then one of them was unlucky enough to escape into self-determination for a while in the time left between the tragic recognition and the lugubrious terminus. Often they escaped into the backwater woods beyond the Flypaper Towns, where their curious brand of whimsical fatalism got mixed up in a white wedding with the hard-bitten, deranged realism of the unreconstructed outlaw *philosophes*. Several momentary lurches of supposition produced more or less at random by moonshiners, hobos, mechanical squirrels and other marginally intellective creatures of the backwaters and woods comprised, logically speaking, mere decoration and embellishment to the foundational views of the *genius loci* thus established, except in cases of demonic intercession and malignant spellcasting. (See *Intellectual History of the Woods Above the Falls*, by Abbot Renego Hodown, esp. chaps. IV & VII.)

# STARK AND SHAGGY

Thunder busted loose off north toward
the Pelting Villages. Loops of storm racket echoed.
Ghosts morphed. Then once more
they fell silent, those old spellwebbed woods.
A will-o'-the-wisp flickered through
the glade, riding an anamorphosed free
radical dust mote. In the middle distance
midges' wings mischievously shimmered.
Mechanical lemurs chattered high in the trees,
swinging on long limber arms between light and dark
patches in the upper irradiated branches.
A pine cone dropped. Stark and shaggy
as thought balloons of Big Foot
several loose wig bubbles drifted
above the benighted hero's shattered vizor.
From the deep woods issued a far-off fluid
rustling sound: perhaps it was a poisoned-
organ-saturated stream rushing between the lost
centuries that now passed the stupid hero by for good.

# MADNESS AND EXILE

Big Jesus went out in the woods around the old abandoned cracking plant near Slate Lake, and encountered a whiskey-drinking Indian named Ira Hayes, who became his informant and taught him the ropes were getting frayed that held together the moonshiner and hobo clans in those woods; that was why everyone and everything was always falling apart; you could look it up in the several annals of clan history. They sat on a tree trunk, taking turns playing on a mouth harp and weeping like babies over the troubles they had known.

The whiskey-drinking Indian had a little trick he did. He would pretend to be throwing back a big slug from a crockery jug that didn't exist. It was pure pantomime, all beautiful wishful thinking, yet sad too. He would blow a cracked blues run on the harp, then pass the imaginary jug on over to Big Jesus. Big Jesus would take his turn, hooking the invisible receptacle with his index finger and throwing back a fake swig. Only the bush-birds and the squirrels were there to see this poignant show, and even they were able to observe but dimly. There wasn't much light shining through the trees, but in those woods that didn't amount to a definite signal of it being either day or night.

The whiskey-drinking Indian handed Big Jesus the mouth harp. He tipped back his prophet's head and produced a riff that penetrated so deep into those woods it set off a mournful echo, melancholy, resonant and strange. A sympathetic pine cone snapped to provide casual syncopation. A flock of tiny bustling tufted something-birds who were busily nibbling on some hanging limes in the upper branches of a sunken mildewed nuthead elm stopped and harkened. It was a moment that had never come before and would never come again in time.

Big Jesus cast his good blue eye up into that tree, and the hanging limes, surprised to be seen there, blinked back at him, preternaturally green. His wandering grey eye rounded up a whole passing batch of throstles and tentatively identified them, also, as possible hanging limes.

Somewhere off in the wilder part of the woods a mechanical owl hooted abstrusely, perhaps in response to his mouth harp wail, and that set off a distant flurry of two-headed dog howls, spooky enough if you were merely encountering them in a legend, even scarier in actuality. It was a moment that had never come before but in these woods was liable to come again, almost any time.

# BIG JESUS PERFORMS THE SEVERAL CEREMONIAL ABLUTIONS

Big Jesus went swimming in Lake Insanity, where even the fish don't go, and came out covered all in mud, as though he'd been swimming in Mud Lake. He took it as a sign he was not really insane, after all, and should go and bathe in Mud Lake. He struck out for Mud Lake. He walked through the woods three days and three nights, and when he got there he waded out in the muddy water, felt dizzy, toppled over, and landed face down in six inches of primeval slime.

In this manner he restored himself in his ritual aspect as the Man of Mud; and when he had revived, he chewed upon pit-banana leaves for strength, until he was able to move on.

# THE HERO DISCOVERED IN HIS
# PATHETIC RITUAL ASPECT

So stripped bare and cleansed, he would
have had cause to hope for better—yet
nobody could help feeling sorry
at the sight that would have greeted them
had they seen him then. When they approached
so close that his condition
grew distinct, grief would have been wrung
from formerly curious eyes.
He appeared clothed in prickly hair
of some poor slain woods animal.
He supported himself by leaning against
the bank of a mud puddle, his head
sunk upon his shoulder like a blind man's
from whom heaven denies its bounty
by piercing his eyes and stitching them
up with iron wire, as once was done
in times of legend
with unquiet mechanical hawks.
Up from the mud puddle sprang vivid
tiger moths and butterflies in abundance,
which brought forth stupid tears
squeezed out between the hero's sewn-up eyelids
as the toll the ritual exacted.

163

# GONE NATIVE

ig Jesus had been gone native so long by this time nobody in Central Falls or for that matter any of the Flypaper Towns could have supplied you with his whereabouts on a bet. Some folks said he was holed up in a Secret Shack somewhere above the Falls, but that was what folks said any time somebody from the Pelting Villages who was gone but not much missed came under discussion. Commentators on Big Jesus' actions as the Man of Mud in the period of madness and exile have worried over the paradox of his mythic significance growing by leaps and bounds even as his specific identity dwindled away to an obscure dark personhood and his individual existence was swept under the rug at the Who Cares Home for Old Knightly Elders up by the blue locks of Bleak Lake, but this is mere persiflage which cannot obscure the facts: in the dark, like a curious flytrap, his legend consumed great swarms of no-see-ums and grew strong, as though they were nutrients.

He endured a lot. He was naked, but in the sultry days of late summer, clothing was optional in those woods anyhow. He ate nuts and berries, pit-banana leaves and hanging limes. Still he waxed lean and poor of flesh, though it was of no concern to him.

He fell in with some poor country hobos who cooked hot dogs over a twig fire by a little muddy stream. They didn't hold him in any particular esteem, but they allowed him his own roasting stick. Whenever he was around they were purposefully low and common in their conversation, and if he attempted to say anything, they would comment sarcastically, Now *that's* clever, and beat him about the head and shoulders, lightly, with their several roasting sticks. That smarted some, him being naked. They took crude means to him. They used blunt shears stolen from a nearby barn to clip his hair and beard down to a rough stubble. He looked way foolish, and they laughed at him. But this was all an extension of the ritual scorn-greeting cere-mony, as he could not but have ascertained.

# PURGATION AND BEWITCHING

Purgation and bewitching
began for the hero after the melancholy
of overnaming that brought on
his muteness in the wake of his Fall from Grace
and before the atrophy of the supernatural
in women that came about with the passing
out of this world of the living
of his main squeeze the chanteuse Nivene—her name
the magic word made by the sound of a mind
pouring concrete into the empty form
of that abyss of curious prattle—
the word *Nivene* in witch-language

# BEYOND THE TREELINE

Beyond the dark treeline another two-headed dog, if that's what it was, took to howling. That time of the year the witches were at their night rituals. The night before, Earl Pudd's cows had strayed out in the green-lit alleged alien-landing-strip meadows near Madder Lake, and the witches had all ganged up over there taunting those poor cows with complex spells termed *moolight maddenings* in the *Ancient Annal of the Spooks*. Refreshed by these exploits, the witches now reassembled up by the Secret Shacks. They surrounded the ceremonial fire circles as mechanical owls were mounted on poles and fuses lit. Then when the insensible animals flared up, the witches taunted and tormented them with their full repertoire of hex yodels, known as the Elder Moo spells. These curious untranslatable ditties, with the deep-memory images of ancient bovine illumination, blood sacrifice, and ritual laser surgery, were dark, deep, alternately solemn and celebratory, entirely dissonant and passing strange. The sonic ensemble created by the spells echoing against the metallic pain-hoots of the burning owls was, at any distance, very difficult for an outsider like Big Jesus to differentiate from a two-headed dog howl, being no expert in such things.

# OUTSIDE THE CHAIN LINK FENCE OF THE SECRET SHACKS

The woods around him were weirdly irradiated, electrical
dismal, bright in patches, dazzling then changing to
pretty deep, dark and passing strange.
Through the forest canopy the toxic sun blazed,
turning the leaves silver brilliant one minute,
the next a blinding matte black. The hero, stupid,
stumbled on in his spellbound waking dream.
It was in those woods the Keepers of the Secret Shacks
had forged the Spell dubbed "Destroyer of Worlds,"
tested it on animals and so turned them
into machines. Their name was Legion.
They swam in charged pools and chattered from stunted trees.
Into those woods the hero stumbled, stupid
if not senseless. Wonder not at the disappearance
of Nivene, for the "Destroyer of Worlds"
is like a wand which upon contact with life
magically deadens it into legend.

# SUNDOWN IN THE WOODS

pells as powerful as a tidal undertow pulled Big Jesus deeper and deeper into those dismal woods. Now we begin to be able or at least inclined to interpret the golden leading strings of the fable as chains of actual lead, the witches of the legend as wishes hatched out of despair, and the mud and slime that be-spatter the tale as so many squished-down flakes of pure, driven snow, stridden upon by lost, confused Knights of yore wandering naked in dismounted ignominy across the rumpus-room viewscreen of amused, unconcerned gods.

Sometimes at twilight in the woods Big Jesus would find his wandering grey eye flitting off up into the lofty top of a venerable bald-crowned alder, where the last rays of the dying sun had been orphaned, while he himself, below on the ground, dwelt in obscurity with his good blue prophet's eye, which though still loyal could do no more for him than the helpless older sibling of a wayward child can do to save their endangered parent.

# THOSE FOOLISH THINGS

Everyone in the forest couldn't help hearing when
Big Jesus started to babble to himself
His obsession with the word *Nivene*
Bound him to say those foolish little things
Which made the elders send down upon him
The disintegrating melancholy overnaming
Always produces in those who speak too soon
In defense of the supernatural in women

# BIG JESUS' DREAM OF THE COLLAPSING PIER

He became a man who has leapt overboard from a departing ship, hanging on to the stanchions of the pier to resist the overpowering pull of the tide. The stanchions were Nivene's thighs. He couldn't see her face, only the saffron bubble of her hair around a head that was pale, blue and ghostly. The tide was dragging him out to sea, she offered the only hope of support. Instead of steadying him, however, she too yielded to the intensity of his need. The power of the undertow pulled them both down. Together they fought against the current, bobbing up, falling back. After struggling like that for a while, they ran out of strength and collapsed together into the yawning deep, no longer resisting it. He decided to set out for shore and began to swim, carving the water with long, desperate strokes. She stayed put, thrashing around in a vain effort to stay afloat. The last time he looked back over his shoulder, her head had disappeared, a pink moon swallowed up by the black waves.

# STUMBLING THROUGH THE WOODS THE HERO LOOKS BACK AND WONDERS

Beauty became dumb by dying-time
and when the memories came swimming in
dolphins with bobbing noses they seemed
with the moonlight shining on their themes—
were those my thoughts dispersing again
like great shoals of midnight herring
when no one's there to ship them into the boat
or were they merely my missing words?

# IN THE FOREST DEEP

He grew fainter than the palest page of the most colorless book. In sleep he thought his errant eye spied the road that would lead him through the thickest darkness of the woods, and then out. Waking, no matter how far and wide he wandered, his true eye never found it. The passageways were dense, overgrown, confusingly bifurcated at critical junctions. Half-blind, his body broken out in sores, his tongue tied in knots, his ears plugged up with mud, he stumbled deeper and deeper into the darkest regions of doubt and mystery at the heart of the forest. From where he was now, down looked like up, yet up appeared to be down, whereas out felt exactly like around and around—though, again, he couldn't be sure about any of it. He no longer recalled the feeling of emerging out of darkness into sunshine, and having his body pleasantly warmed. He covered himself with mud to keep from freezing as the days grew shorter and dimmer, the nights sharper and more prolonged. The going got difficult, and then the going got more difficult, and so on, and so on.

This whole Forest Deep part of the legend is so familiar to some people from the seasonal liturgies as to demand brevity in the retelling. Hearing it again may be a little like throwing a sprig of sunken mildewed nuthead elm bough on the fire, and dropping the needle on an old disc of two-headed-dog-howl recordings from the archival mechanical-animal field studies of the Millennial Period.

Familiarity with the legend, however, shouldn't be allowed to vitiate the impact of certain recognitions, at this point.

Big Jesus Toomer, as a veritable person, remained, in the ambient swill of real life, a mere crooked-eyed doofus hillbilly mutant on a mission, with a romantic nature and a rapidly developing sociopathic streak, who would have been better off without that mission (given all the pain his failure to save mankind had caused him and everyone), without that nature (given all the grief that was the legacy of his plunge into romance), and without that streak (given the retributiveness of any society, even one so deficient in perceptual retention as that depicted in this legend).

Weirdly enough, though, even at this late stage of the proceedings he had his good blue eye, much of the time, and however belatedly, on a guiding star, albeit one dwelling now only inside his mind.

The aforementioned star—before being ripped by his own hand from the sky, on a night when his wandering eye had got ahold of him—had possessed a veritable face, blueish, pale, ghostly, attenuated, frantic-eyed, and surrounded by a burst-bubble of Madder Lake-style ritual tresses that shone, in death as in life, vivid as an exploding rose-pink supernova; though the description just given cannot be confirmed with any certainty, given the inadequate lighting of the Forest Deep.

# UNBEKNOWNST TO HIM,
# NIVENE PURSUES THE LOST HERO
# INTO THE ANIMISTIC HEART OF
# THE FOREST DEEP

As anxiety in the face of death
walks hand in hand through the Forest Deep
with anxiety in the face of life,
the chanteuse travels after him, not quite
alone. Like a golden
tone hurrying through thick silence in
search of its darker overtones,
accompanied yet friendless she hastens,
chased by revenant souls
of butterfly simulacra, wing-
heavy with overnaming, redolent
of the mud, feces and rotting earth-smells
of their mute mechanic birth. As she goes
she chants old rude open vowels
of extinct witch-orders, showing she knows
at the heart of the woods lies chaos.

# HUMILITY

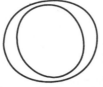nce he was in the heart of the Forest Deep, Big Jesus took inventory. Since practically everything he had was gone, it required no more than a moment or two.

Some yellow-tufted squirrels and bush-birds had been tagging along after him for fun. He walked with them, grumbled and growled with them, called them his own, and left to them his last shoe lace, a bequest of some significance. He had anyway only saved it to tie around his finger in the event he had something he wanted to remember, and now his object was to forget everything. The squirrels and bush-birds, however, were utterly and completely lacking in memory function. They used the shoe lace to tie up a semi-comatose puppet-dwarf, Ufa Thup-Person, who'd been snoozing-off a bout with a moonshine jug under a sunken mildewed nuthead elm. Big Jesus made them untie him. The thoughtless little pranksters sniggered and chafed a bit, but soon complied, swayed by his great patience and gentleness.

Intense waves of migraine assailed Big Jesus around this time, probably caused by gross toxic spell uptake. Reverberations rocked his brain container. Still he took these changeling children of the forest unto his mud-covered breast, and traced his finger over each small scar and ding and dent thereon, recounting the several trials and tribulations these wounds represented. The squirrels and bush-birds and other critters attended intermittently, as the woods grew calm. They gathered round his unshod feet, and wondered tremendously at his grumbles.

A flock of blue-tufted something-birds vacated their comfortable perch in the upper boughs of a venerable bald-crowned alder in order to follow him. They were thirsty, and to each of them he gave a single drop of brambleberry juice, in thus wise sharing out the last of his potables.

His stock of provisions now amounted to a few scraps of stale bread, the gift of some itinerant hobo sage. By virtue of these he had been tenuously maintaining himself. He now bestowed them upon some lost and hungry-looking speckled doves he had bumped into while wandering in a dry scrub gully.

Afterwards he felt a curious weightlessness of a sort he'd never previously experienced. Then a great shining speckled dove appeared to him in a bramble bush. For a moment he felt uplifted. It was a kind of selfless elation he had felt once before, in the Knights' locker room, when the little band of varsity starters, be-grimed and sweat-glimmering in their ancient helmets and pads after their great victory over the Madder Lake Crimson Twisters in the sectional championship game, formed a circle and joined hands to utter in unison the vow of mutual allegiance. Then came the ceremonial Brain Bonding. The sharp clash of skulls butting together in the excitement of unison cranial collision would echo inside each of them, down through the years, even when they had all gone out on several roads of life, each to his own particular path. That of Earl Pudd had led him into Moolight. That of Aggro Vayne had led him into lordly pelf. That of Big Jesus Toomer had led him into these woods, where a curious great shining speckled bird was eyeing him kindly from a bramble bush. The bird had a brilliant eye of blue crystal, which shone through the hanging clusters of ripe brambleberries like a tiny turquoise flashlight beam hidden among purple grapes.

# A WALK IN THE WOODS NEAR THE ABBEY
# OF THE WITCHES SUPERIOR

Amid the humble beams of moolight
Big Jesus tumbled to the source
of the great shrieks and sighs and groans
and howls and grumbles that arose
out of the deep woods all around him
even when he clapped his calloused feelers
over his horny prophet's ears. The Force
had grown into a Time Ghost, womanish,
witchy-haired and slender. She walked with him,
talked with him and called him her own.
Which is superior, isolation
or muddy intercourse with phantoms
that haunt the irrational noise trees
planted here by elders long weird eons ago
to animate their lifeless spells?

# THE FORCE

Mysterious is the force that drives arrogance to call down fate, challenge it with dignified courage, battle against it with varying fortunes; this force is not abandoned by the legend without hope of bringing a new law to mankind in the long run. Although the legend brings the wrath of toxic spellbinding down upon the hero as punishment, it stops short of claiming his life; it leaves him behind on the lacustrine shore, outlined against the horizon, upright upon the banks of Lake Plantagenet, stark, iconic, strange, a kind of jagged boundary stone on the frontier between animal and mechanical, sentient and nescient, past and future. Justice, not truth, is the principle of all legendmaking.

Big Jesus had by this time threaded his way through a strip of singularly mean country, past several terrible tarns, up four terminal moraines, down six mist-cloaked gulches, across eleven muddy creeks and over nine dank scrub hollows, as far as the shadowy wooded margins of the central Forest Deep, coming finally to a point demarcated by the ancient cartographers with a black cross representing the ill-fated former settlement of Outer Spite. All of this terrain is liberally splotched on those old maps by cautionary patches of delicate grey and green crosshatching, indicating areas of potential toxic spell exposure, with small pale numerals coded to accompanying key lists specifying spell type, half-life, etc.

And to speak true, these exhaustive and exhausting wanderings had taken their considerable toll on the former Knight.

A sympathetic response to nocturnal howls of madness he seemed to hear emanating from a pink moon that rose without variation to his left and remained on his left no matter which way he turned, night after night, triggered an inner ear imbalance that made it difficult for him to take two steps without falling over. A marked sensation of hyper-irreality resulting from spatial disorientation gave him small fits. Introduced on one occasion to a stranger, he shook hands not with the person but with the person's shadow, while apparently overlooking the figure who had cast it. He complained to several rambling backwoods witch-doctors of ataraxia, xerostomata, acromegaly, manual hirsutism, and sudden growth spurts in his canines, but they advised him nothing could be done. He lost motor control for days at a time, often felt like a certain sickly yellow-tufted squirrel was inhabiting his body, and when suddenly confused was prone to begin vomiting and weeping at the same time.

His wandering grey eye took advantage of bouts of unexpected movement and double vision in his good blue prophet's eye to try to put all sorts of little hallucinations over on him, like multiplying stale loaves and broken-winged flying fishes, all phantasmal, in wicker baskets placed high in the limbs of pit-banana trees. He suffered too, and oft full grievously, from bleeding foot, tremor, hearing loss, and an unfortunate facial edema that caused his head to swell up like a pumpkin and pain him accordingly. He felt at almost all times a heavy dull feeling upon his chest, and at night hallucinated the body of a dead woman was being pressed upon him.

His liver swelled up on him. His gums grew sore and puffy. His urine was hard in fetching, his tongue coated with a fine white dust. Strange malaises would frequently sweep over him like clouds of poison gas on the more fetid backwoods nights, and then later on, when the first deep cold snaps hit, he experienced a racing heartbeat and finally awoke early one chilly morning from an insomniac's nightmare of rolling dice for the holy grail with his eyelids stuck together by a curious dark grey substance that seemed to be descending over the woods, like airborne granulated lava.

Soon thereafter, in the selflessness of legendmaking, he stopped sleeping altogether.

# SLEEPLESSNESS AND NIVENE

As leafy senators of the forest knew
this whole time the ghost Nivene
who lived in the hero's spellbound mind
had a lot of trouble getting her rest
for every time the camp fire snapped
in the grate of her refrigerated heart
as she pursued him through the forest
the heaviness of sleep was torn
by a blast of poor perdu
dressed up as molten lava
and tears turned to poisoned medicine
on her lips as she stooped to kiss him in
her own image in that burning pool

# THE LETTER

ig Jesus lived in a time of his own this entire time. The phantom voice of the chanteuse was in his ear with every breath he breathed. But he was now hellbent on either collapsing or escaping time, even if it meant stopping breathing. Sometimes he would let out a great symptomatic Knightly rebel yell into the Forest Deep, but the content of it always came out strange and twisted. The venerable trees sighed. For days at a time he pretty much lost the ability to form words, as those old leafy senators knew.

Some drifter who bumped into him down in a scrub hollow on his hands and knees grubbing for slugs mistook him at first for a crazed religious hermit, then recognized him as a toxic spell victim, took pity on him, and carried away a letter. The letter was addressed, curiously enough, to Zeke Toomer, his dead twin brother.

The letter had been written for Big Jesus by a puppet-dwarf actually named Jeremy Bentham-Thup, but called Dinadan by the hobos and moonshiners of the woods because they mistook his name to be Dan, and he often stayed for dinner.

Dinadan offered his letter-writing services gratis because Big Jesus appeared mighty sad, and Dinadan had little else to offer. He had stumbled upon Big Jesus in a scrub gulch. Big Jesus was pretty bent out of shape, all right. He was eating some straw and sniffling. But he cheered up at the prospect of writing a letter to his dead twin brother, who had been occasionally in his thoughts. Moreover he had put out the whole light of the past over the door of a certain dark horse, to which he now knew he would have to return for the night, bearing a full bucket of toxic oats.

While Big Jesus dictated the letter, Dinadan fell asleep. But since Big Jesus was unable to speak, there were no words to be taken down. He dictated the whole letter in his heart, to his mind, which was also sleeping. Afterwards he felt refreshed and greatly consoled. Then he dozed off again.

Dinadan awoke, and for the sake of completeness, wrote down a number of words. Dawn broke, and a mechanical owl hooted off in the woods somewhere. Or perhaps it was twilight, which in those woods often seemed very much the same.

Big Jesus forgot his letter to his dead brother completely, and never laid a wandering eye on the puppet-dwarf Dinadan again.

# THE SELF-UNSEEING
## (IMAGINARY LETTER TO NIVENE)

Dear Nivene, I'll tell you, life and death
could never shake my manhood
as much as these hot tears that burst
from my fond eyes onto this paper, when I think
this paper in my imagination
on which I'm writing this letter to you
as if you were my flesh and blood
is actually the deed that keeps
my errant eyes on either side of my nose
as I walk through this black space
in propinquity to myself, like a blind person.

# THE BOOKS OF BIG JESUS

The weeks and months he spent alone with himself were crowded by some clamorous phantoms of spell-knowledge, badgering and taunting him until one dark day in those awful woods, in obedience to their inconsiderate commands, he began to compose books in his head, merely to appease them, and give due office to their orderings, while he remained their prisoner.

His mental books composed in the woods at that time were mere compilations of mechanical animal lore but were not made without some discrimination. He looked up, and mechanical creatures on every side spoke to him. These he knew to be the incarnate embodiments of thoughts aimed directly into his mind. Suddenly, without warning, he knew something of vacuums and siphoning. The knowledge was there, in his mind, and could not be taken away from him.

The mechanical animals that were sent to him told him unspeakable things about the spell-sequestered *hims, hers* and *its*, poor naked wretches kept in suspended animation in frozen vapor tanks sunk deep beneath the unfathomed bottom of Lake Insanity. Big Jesus listened to all that was reported to him. He rejected certain stories, but accepted others, for example the story of the mechanical barnacle-goose growing on trees deep in the heart of the forest. Then there was the story that the average mechanical lynx had such keen sight that it could see through nine walls. The voices told him that this had actually been experimentally verified by showing that such and such a lynx, with nine walls between it and an Elder-appointed animal trainer carrying a piece of meat, always stopped, when the experimenter stopped, at a point exactly opposite the meat, which gave Big Jesus pause.

Around then he began to exhibit signs of circularity in his

behavior. Every day he went back to where he'd left off the day before and thrashed around a little, then fell back exhausted. Lost in the woods, but where? In our imagination?

Tongues of flame disturbed the cool path of a snail across his spellbound gaze. He looked up and saw a mechanical flamingo standing on one leg, staring at him. It was one of those serene waterwalkers that travel over the lakes like slow schooners for a while, then are snatched down to submerged power stations where they are reprogrammed in the absentminded arts of the submarine depths. For half a beat the whole large cosmos paused, shrank, grew infinitely small.

So things stood, when, stubbornly, a small swarm of horse-bottleflies lifted up off a lily pad and buzzed-out the fanatic frequencies of the mechanical upanishads which announced twilight in those woods.

# THE AWAKENING

Golden rays of sunrise flooded the upper strata of woods. Blood flushed with courage bloomed in the throats of the blue-tufted something-birds, piping their manic songs of imaginary power from the high branches of a venerable bald-crowned alder. The rustling of a distant stream washed away the chill of the night and life awoke, yawned and stretched. Its long spell of pensiveness, obscurity and longing was over. The congealed flames of the sun began once again to stoke up. All things began, once again, to rush, babble and fuse with all things. Above, through a rent in the tall umbrella of trees, a beam of light entered the lower realm, excited friction and conflict in the exiled hero's heart. Within moments, a thought would burst forth.

# THE AWAKENING (II)

And then came the weirdest spell torment of all.
A taped voice was piped into the forest,
a submarine pipe-knock ancient radio
voice of heraldic knightly history,
narrating the hero's immortal senior year
open field run against the Two-Headed Dogs.
The broadcast echoed through the forest deep,
it reverberated with the Oh Nos and Holy Cows
of the most passing strange elements
in the legend. The whole forest briefly stopped
breathing—mechanical owls, curious,
peered imperiously into space,
listening. *He sits frozen and motionless,*
that ancient commentator lamented.
*Now he's thrown the ball. It instantly*
*calls him back to life. He leaps to his feet.*
*He hops. He swerves. He runs. He dribbles*
*the ball with a truly acrobatic genius.*
*He throws it up, he catches it with the tip of one foot,*
*he kicks it up, he catches it, he kicks it up again,*
*he juggles the football with one foot,*
*he hops the entire length of the field,*
*fans! He hardly shows any normal activity,*
*only this bizarre and spasmodic*
*activity! It's a touchdown!*

The tinny cheering of the crowd drowned
out all sounds in the woods for a moment,
and the naked hero lay back on a clump of mud,
his head reeling with a sick pain as he understood
for the first time his whole knightly career
had been spell-directed.

188

None of his heroics belonged to him,
everything had been made up elsewhere.
This knowledge came as a rude awakening.

# THE ASPHODEL

A couple of interrogation-scarred puppet-dwarves were sitting around throwing down black mugs of spoiled animal-water in a house of ill repute named after the Flower of Death up at Freeport, on Mud Lake, when there appeared in the doorway a scraggly, dodgy-looking stranger with a stringy prophet's beard and one rambling eye. The stranger dragged himself inside out of the rain, shook off water like a big dog, and said, Outside that door this moment has never been before, within this door this moment will never come again. The proprietress handed the fellow a bowl of overripe fruit with withered leaves, pushed him into an armchair and told him to cool his heels while one of the girls painted his portrait in heroic colors. You look like a regular Knight, she volunteered provocatively. The deathly sad wantonness of the place tore his ritual soul open, exposing what remained of his dark, beating heart. So this was the Abyss of Sex, which now tired him exceedingly. Then, like an asphodel, the Abyss of Sex closed up again. And the force of arrogance that had called down fate severed itself from the golden leading strings, permitting him to turn at last toward death and home.

# THE HERO'S DREAM OF ATTEMPTING
# TO TRAP AND BOTTLE
# THE UNTOUCHABLE PURITY OF NIVENE

It's the single night of love before death,
the night of renunciation,
the path blocked through possession
of a woman. The hero, stunned, must
turn away and find a new
path out of the poisoned garden,
hurling net, bag, bottle and broken
specimen rudely to the ground,
that predestined grave of spirit,
where Nivene's shattered wings,
long, pointed and discal,
flicker like a delphinium
in a clump of thistles—
the light minimal, the dark scaling
turning a deeper blue ochre
with the dying of the evening,
and then a silvery white.

# 8. The Day of Destiny

# A CLEARING (NIVENE REAPPEARS)

Wings thinly scaled in postmedian light
appear transparent. The one last
isolated colony is about to die out.
Alighting on a bright patch of reeking mud,
she holds her wings over her back,
turning toward the small patch of sun,
and leans to the side, so that
the shadow she casts is minimized.
In this way she's protected.

# AMONG THE STONES

The Elders' bell tolled for vespers rituals, and as the last golden cloud sank down into the far horizon over the great grave bluffs west of the Falls, blue evening came on under the old pines and alders, calling its motherless children home.

A small breeze ran gentle silver fingers through the matted, tangled mane of the homecoming son, Big Jesus Toomer, wandering at twilight in the old Central Falls graveyard. Things hadn't changed much here, he mused, since those deep past practice dusks of yesteryear, when he had rough-housed and rambled between the stately plots of the forefathers, pounding longnecks and carousing under the pit-banana-leaf harvest-pink moon with the Vayne brothers, Buddy and Aggro, while the Brotherhood of the Knights still lived. Perhaps, he figured, phantoms of their own youthful souls were among the many ancient presences that now almost palpably flitted through the gloaming among the clouds of insensible no-see-ums that were diving and swarming over the stones, doomed to surrender their lives with the dying of the day yet blissfully unaware of it, because ecstatically multiplying a mile a minute.

The bare quorum of brain cells that had managed to survive Big Jesus' several quests and trials had at this eleventh hour assembled into something like a conscious motive: the finding of the stones of those who lay in restless wait for him, their several scores unsettled. This his once good blue prophet's eye, now cracked and glazed, found itself called upon to execute as a last earthly mission. Beneath one of those stolid markers, old Ma Toomer, an endarkened blob of absence, wrestled with the importunate shades; another stone crushed down the miserable sod that covered the bones of Nivene. A toxic-spellbound butterfly, animated entirely by spirits in its death throes, fluttered in the last rays of daylight lightly dusting the bald crown of a venerable yellow alder. The shimmering creature caught up his wandering grey eye, so that as he milled among the stones the wig bubbles were drifting, drifting away on its fragile iridescent wings.

# APPROACHING METAMORPHOSIS

Toward the end of his program the hero felt
As if he were approaching metamorphosis–
Perhaps the last foolish emotion
He would ever feel, as dissolution joined
Metaphor to reveal *larval*
(In his case) as a stage in degeneration,
And the hollow husk he was now to leave
Behind (thinking stupidly of that shed
Integument as part of interesting pupa
History) as a glittering death
Mask. Mischievous as a midge's wing
In the increasingly spellclouded
Field of vision that remained to him,
A revived Nivene materialized, changing
Back into herself.

# ANAMORPHOSIS
## (THE DOUBTFUL RESOLUTION OF THE REVERSAL-OF-ROMANCE QUEST CRUX)

T he witch commentator Bava Smythe-Thup, in her monograph on magical anamorphosis, got three things right. The geography of legend is wet and flat. The swamp country between grudge and desire remains to be dredged. And the tale of the terrible culmination of a reversal-of-romance quest is never easily related. When the unspeakable occurs, mythic subjects are often rendered voiceless. But couldn't they have spoken, had they found the words? Then again, weren't the words, too, as bewitched in the many subterranean intertanglings of their several tellings as their originating events, by the mere legend-complicating circumstance of having happened? Over the eons variorum clung to and mingled with variorum, down through the grainy-filtered epochs, until only a tenuous, fragile lacework precipitate of the first violent seed-spilling story remained even marginally to be trusted.

Anamorphic distortion, according to Abbot Squayre Dood, always causes the twisted to turn out straight and the bent to show up true, in the old funhouse-mirror histories. Yet it's also a fact, as everyone knows, that in reviewing old histories the distorting-glass of our minds habitually sends the broken fragments of language that come in to us back to their seeming ancient senders with the mixed messages ironed-out into shocking simplicities. What indeed could have told Big Jesus more about any one-dimensional truth, at that moment, than the monsters crouching in wait in concealed corners of his own spellbound imagination—those incorrigible creations of his hex-crossed mind, with their blinding mysteries now at last to be exposed to him?

# THE DAY OF DESTINY

The Chapel Terrible stood in a small hollow between two tall old sunken mildewed nuthead elms. As Big Jesus approached, a little bell somewhere tinkled. Lightning struck, a tree fell. There was a sound of heavy lumbering. Big Jesus could sense the life draining out of him. His limbs felt stiff and the heavy lumbering he heard when the little bell tinkled was in fact nothing but the dull, loud pounding of his overexerted heart.

His last quest compelled him up the three broad marble steps to the great bronze chapel doors. A stubby, balding sub-abbot admitted him and ushered him through those vast imposing portals, down an antechamber lined with rows of small dark cages, into a stone-walled inner sanctum that held several long glass cases, dimly lit from within, where the Red Books and Blood-Smirched Cleats of the Ancient Knights were on display.

A silent, subdued monk led him by the shaky arm up to a text-stand in the center of the room, pointed a bony finger to a line on the page of a book that lay open there, and then fled off into the shadows.

Above the text-stand a small screen flashed blank squares of flat color; as the squares slowly merged, letters and words began forming. Big Jesus leaned forward to apply his tired blue prophet's eye to the line of text that was unscrolling: *This moment has never come before*, it said. In that instant the terrestrial visage of Nivene floated up on the screen. The ghost girl smiled at him rather coolly from a suspicious distance that would have seemed excessively remote had she not always kept it, stifled a nervous little laugh, and then began to sing:

> *Put my photo in the fridge,*
> *Ice me till I'm cubic.*
> *By the frozen river*

**200** ॐ

*Doofus voodoo chills me.*
*I see that blue light flashing.*
*What's there to do but pray.*

The voice and image faded away, vanishing back into the elusive artificial space of the Compressorium, where the inner drive-bank that powered the Secret Shacks was housed. Big Jesus heard vague rustling sounds behind him. Three witches had come in, holding simulated torches. He turned to go but they said, all together and in their curious singsong way, No, No, you really must not go. Stay, stay, you must not go away. And he felt all the power to leave being sucked out of him.

A large, hulking sub-abbot, partially disfigured by a great scar that zigzagged across his low forehead before disappearing down one thick, crooked brow, came in slowly swinging a censer which puffed out dense clouds of aromatic smoke. Several other witches and monks also filed into the room, which was now getting kind of crowded. A low, gruff chanting started up. The words seemed to be in a language Big Jesus didn't understand. The air grew suffocatingly thick and he felt his knees wobbling. The wig bubbles phased into automatic drift, as though suspecting the end was near. At this point, one by one, the ritual celebrants began exiting, still mumbling their enigmatic chant. Finally the room was quiet and the only living soul who remained in it with him was a pale, frizzy-haired waif of a girl in a snood who had caught the attention of his wandering grey eye by emerging, toward the end of the ceremony, from a coffin that had appeared on the text screen. Now fully materialized, she turned, bent over as gracefully as a young alder giving way to a funnel cloud wind, peered down into the screen with her pale blue eyes, and saw the good blue eye of Big Jesus staring out at her for the last time.

# NIVENE'S DREAM

Big sad-faced parallel infinity
I cried into your false twilight
a moon cupped in your creamwhite hands
poured milky awareness over me
more to feed my dream than to drown my fear
my tears blurry with repetitiveness
pearly sand grains scattered over that
whole opening into night like out through
the motion of that two-way mirror
where those planets open into that ocean

(that ocean

you

# Postlude: The Spell

# THE SPELL

The day of the dead when
the veil between us and them
is thinnest          eyelash
kitty breath          umbrella flutter
psychic butterfly—

A whole procession of them coming
pushing through the thin
mesh of the net—the sugar candy
shedding of the skin and how
it lets the wind blow through the veins
the dance of the skulls and when
the spinning of the little mechanic
inside the toy clock stops
the dark man carrying two suitcases
steps from the now no longer
moving train—

That's the day when
I know someone will be
no longer waiting,
the unborn child said.
I invented what I wanted to say
in case anybody out there,
on a cold grey day in autumn,
wanted to hear the thoughts
of the dead—

I opened the door and
in flew a moth, thinking
*twilight came early*

Printed May 2000 in Santa Barbara &
Ann Arbor for the Black Sparrow Press by
Mackintosh Typography & Edwards Brothers Inc.
Text set in ITC-Garamond and Empire by Words Worth.
Design by Barbara Martin.
This first edition is published in paper wrappers;
there are 200 hardcover trade copies;
100 hardcover copies have been numbered &
signed by the author; & 22 copies lettered A–V
have been handbound in boards by
Earle Gray, each with an original
drawing by Tom Clark.

TOM CLARK grew up in Chicago, where as a young man he ushered at public events featuring such figures of the era as Joe DiMaggio, Sugar Ray Robinson, Bobby Hull, Ted Williams, Ernie Banks and Harry S Truman. He graduated in 1963 from the University of Michigan and did postgraduate studies in England at the Universities of Cambridge and Essex. In the 1960s he began editing poetry publications small and large, from the free-radical *Once* series of mimeographed books and magazines to *The Paris Review* (serving as poetry editor from 1963 to 1973). Over the years he has worked variously as a teacher, writer, critic and artist. He has published his poetry in such collections as *Stones, Air, John's Heart, At Malibu, When Things Get Tough on Easy Street, A Short Guide to the High Plains, Paradise Resisted, Disordered Ideas, Fractured Karma, Sleepwalker's Fate,* and *Like Real People*; poetry mingles with history in *Empire of Skin*, an account of the Northwest Coast fur trade, and with biography in *Junkets on a Sad Planet*, a verse life of John Keats. Biography also provides the major form of many of his books in prose, including *Late Returns: A Memoir of Ted Berrigan, Jack Kerouac, Robert Creeley and the Genius of the American Common Place,* and *Charles Olson: The Allegory of a Poet's Life.* Among his books containing writings on and images of sports and popular culture are *The World of Damon Runyon, Champagne and Baloney, One Last Round for the Shuffler, Fan Poems* and *Baseball.* His works of fiction include a volume of tales, *The Last Gas Station*, and three novels, *Who Is Sylvia?, The Exile of Céline,* and *The Spell* (parts of which have been recorded in a collaborative project with the musician/composer Clark S. Nova, under the title *Doofus Voodoo*). His literary essays and reviews have appeared in *The New York Times, Times Literary Supplement, Los Angeles Times, San Francisco Chronicle, London Review of Books,* and many other journals.